A Halloween Tale

Austin Crawley

A Halloween Tale
by
Austin Crawley

First published in Great Britain in 2019
by **Provisioners Press**
Kindle Edition

Copyright Austin Crawley 2019

CONTENTS

"That is not dead which can eternal lie, And with strange aeons even death may die. The oldest and strongest emotion of mankind is fear, and the oldest and strongest kind of fear is fear of the unknown.

The most merciful thing in the world, I think, is the inability of the human mind to correlate all its contents."

~ H.P. Lovecraft

Chapter One

Phillip crept up behind the toad with all of his perceived skill of the ninja warriors in the martial arts movies he loved to watch with his brother. Raymond, the elder of the two, rolled his eyes in derision, but he stood absolutely still so he wouldn't spook his brother's prey. Tesha, Phillip's best friend, looked on with disapproval, yet she, too, remained perfectly still.

Suddenly Phillip leapt into the air in a trajectory meant to bring himself down on top of the toad, where he could curl his body and land on knees and elbows to trap the amphibian. However, the movement alerted the creature to danger and it leapt into the safety of the hedge in front of the house they had been passing. Phillip stretched out mid-flight in an attempt to grasp the escaping animal and landed belly first in a puddle, left over from last night's rain. The murky water splashed his pale-skinned face and school clothes with dark brown mud. Tesha thought she saw wetness in Phillip's dark hair as well.

Rather than helping his brother, Raymond doubled over with laughter.

"Just as well," Tesha admonished, pushing a lock of her long, black hair behind her ear. "Animals are entitled to live in peace. What were you planning to do? Keep it for a pet?"

Phillip rolled out of the puddle and sat up, looking sheepish.

"I was just gonna take it to Amy's Halloween party tomorrow night. Show it around and scare some girls." He winked, flashing his most charming grin at his childhood friend.

"Well I'm glad you didn't catch it." Tesha made no effort to hide her condemnation. "Toads need water. That one probably lives in Mrs. Elwin's pond."

Phillip followed Tesha's glance at the house behind the hedge. Despite the privacy afforded by the Hawthorne bushes, everyone knew that Mrs. Elwin kept a pond with Koi fish in her backyard. She was forever complaining about the ravages of neighborhood cats who didn't respect her boundary fences.

"Besides, it's an all-night party. First one my mother ever let me go to, thanks to you." Tesha flashed a grin at Phillip.

"What do I have to do with it?" Phillip asked.

"Because I promised her you would be there, and you've always looked out for me like a brother. She trusts you."

"What if I get off with someone?"

"You?" Raymond scoffed at his brother. "Since when do you get off with girls? I don't think you even *like* girls!"

"I have a girl for my best friend!" Phillip took a combative stance, as if he would fight his brother for the insult.

"You know what I mean." Raymond scoffed at his brother, ignoring his defensiveness. "You're nearly seventeen and never asked a girl on a date. Are you going to take your best friend to the senior prom next year?" Raymond glanced at Tesha, then resumed walking a little faster than they had been strolling down Hazelwood Avenue before Phillip had delayed them by trying to catch the toad.

Tesha scowled, but kept quiet. Raymond had always rubbed her the wrong way and she got the impression that he didn't much like her, either. She and Raymond had long since developed a habit of mostly ignoring each other, even on their regular walk to school. Besides, she didn't want to be late or to see Phillip argue with his brother. Physically they resembled each other closely, especially the odd greenish-hazel colour of their eyes, but they were very different people. Tesha would never mistake Raymond's incessant moody scowls with Phillip's easy smile and bright, flashing eyes.

Phillip and Tesha jogged to catch up, but Phillip stopped them again when they came to a familiar old house, known locally simply as Number 23 Hazelwood Avenue. The address had become like a label for the place. It had been uninhabited for generations, fallen to county ownership, yet no one had attempted to restore the place and put it up for sale within even their parent's lifetimes.

The old, abandoned house reminded Tesha of a photograph she had once seen, where a single house stood in black and white, surrounded by brightly-painted residences with lush garden foliage and beautiful wisteria trees cascading their purple blooms on either side of the colorless dwelling, as if to frame the only ashy-hued residence on the block. The houses on either side of Number 23 at least had well-tended lawns and flowers growing in front of their windows. Tesha wondered how the contrast looked to Raymond, who was completely colorblind.

"I don't suppose we could convince Amy to hold the party in there," Phillip speculated. "The atmospherics would be wicked!"

Tesha mock-punched him in the arm.

"That's called trespassing. That's why they post security guards on Halloween every year." For just a moment, a wistful expression in her eyes gave away her real feelings on the matter. "I'd love to see the inside, but those kids last Halloween got in real trouble trying to break in."

"They were stupid." Raymond twisted his mouth in disdain. "A bunch of thirteen-year-olds making a lot of noise and trying to crack a window in the front of the house was guaranteed to get caught by one of the guards. They could've at least gone around to the back."

"I hear there's only going to be one guard this year," Phillip mentioned. "There's cut-backs on everything these days."

Tesha glanced at the dry, dead rose vines that covered the sides of the house. Everything on the property looked long since dead and withered, except for the only half-dead, overgrown grass of the front lawn and a tall monkey-puzzle tree sprouting from in front of the left side window.

The house was two storeys, like the other houses on the street, and the tree grew high enough that Tesha could almost imagine climbing down from a bedroom window. She remembered Phillip attempting to climb the tree when they were six. They had been playing in the long grass, hiding within the brown, bent blades that rustled loudly when she moved, no matter how hard she tried to stalk her best friend quietly.

"Do you think it's really haunted like people say?" Phillip asked. "Or is that just a story to keep kids and transients out?"

"Any abandoned house gets a reputation for being haunted," Raymond sneered. "We've been walking past that place all our lives and I haven't seen a spook come out yet."

Tesha smirked at Raymond's comment, a hint of a smile

gleaming in her dark eyes.

"I don't believe in ghosts. The only dangerous thing about that place is that it's condemned and the walls could fall down on your head. I have a Bengali grandma and she's always talking about spirits; ghosts with unfulfilled desires that walk the Earth, but it's all superstition. It's nothing but an old house."

"They should bulldoze that place before it falls on someone's head." Everyone turned at the sound of the deep southern drawl of Joseph Despre, Raymond's friend from the senior class. He trotted up to join them, his dark, Afro-Caribbean skin gleaming in the morning sun. "The place is an insurance nightmare. Jerry Applegate pulled guard duty this year for Halloween and he says there's no way he's steppin' inside, even if there ain't no ghosts."

"I thought he got fired for sleeping on the job?" Raymond screwed up his eyebrows into a confused expression.

"He got a last warning," Joseph explained. "Not that anyone's likely to check up on him."

"I say we go in," Raymond proposed.

"We could get in serious trouble!" Tesha could see her moment of freedom becoming the last time her old world Asian parents trusted her to stay out at night.

"We'll be okay," Phillip assured her. "If we get spotted, we run off in different directions. I'll make sure you're not the one the guard follows."

Phillip's enthusiastic grin had always been difficult to resist. He had been charming teachers with it for years and might have got them both into trouble many times over the years, if he hadn't been so good at squirming out of a tight situation. Tesha's own infinite practicality had helped save them many times. If her parents had any idea of half the stuff she had got up to without getting caught...

"What about you? If you get arrested or something, won't you get grounded?"

"That's the beauty of it," Phillip boasted. "If that happened, you're the one person my parents would let come to see me because you're the good girl who never gets in trouble!"

A laugh escaped her lips and Tesha brought her hand up to her mouth, as if to contain her mirth. Many of her adventures with Phillip were not for Raymond's ears, or Joseph's. Secrets had a way of coming out. After all, it was all innocent fun. Getting into places they shouldn't be, slipping out of class after the role had been taken to meet at the library and read more interesting Classic books to each other than their English teacher ever assigned.

None of their jaunts had risked potentially serious punishment. Leaving an all-night party where she had promised to be at in order to trespass in a potentially hazardous old house was pushing higher stakes.

A deep rumbling sound abruptly stopped all conversation. It seemed to come from the street and only lasted a couple of seconds, but everyone was instantly alert, ready to run for safety if they could determine where it could be found. Raymond was the first to break the silence.

"Was that an earthquake?"

"We don't have earthquakes in this state," Phillip contended.

"There's been some," Tesha corrected him. "Just nothing big enough to notice since 1987."

"Says the straight 'A' geology student!" Phillip returned.

"That just means I know what I'm talking about!"

8

"It came from the house!" Joseph's booming voice broke into the exchange.

"No, man," Raymond cut in. "I went on a student trip to California last year and minor earthquakes are like that. They happen all the time out there. Come on, we're going to be late."

Raymond started striding quickly up the street with Joseph one step behind him, their long legs leaving Phillip and Tesha to walk at their own pace.

"I tell you something came from that house. I saw lights flashing in the upstairs windows!" Joseph's voice trailed as the older boys got further ahead. Tesha and Phillip walked a little faster than before, but Tesha didn't want to catch up with Phillip's brother. They usually had extra time in the morning anyway and if they took their time, they would only miss hanging out with their other friends before home room.

Tesha thought about what Joseph said about flashing lights. Was there a fire hazard in the old house? Surely the electricity would have been turned off long ago. Transients with flashlights maybe? She wondered if they should report it, but Joseph was the only one who had seen anything and she didn't know him well enough to be sending authorities to question him.

"Tesha, what do you think Joseph saw?" Sometimes Tesha thought Phillip could read her mind.

"It could have been a reflection in the window glass. If the earthquake made the glass rattle..."

"Did *you* feel the ground move?" The doubtful expression on Phillip's face made Tesha wonder whether she actually had felt anything, or if her impression of shaking was only from suggestion.

"They say you don't really feel the small ones. I did feel...

9

something. Not shaking exactly, but for a minute it was sort of like... being disoriented. Like everything sort of stretched sideways or something." Tesha shuddered. Putting it into words brought up questions in her mind about what could cause her perceptions to go off-kilter, if only for a moment.

"We're going to be late if we don't hurry." Phillip started walking faster. Tesha took one quick glance at the house behind them and hurried to keep up. She couldn't help thinking that her friend had changed the subject because whatever they had experienced had spooked him.

Just as well, she thought. *We shouldn't even be considering trying to sneak into that old place on Halloween. It was a crazy idea from the start.*

Chapter Two

The young priest, wearing a black cassock, looked out of place sitting across the desk in the town mayor's office, yet disturbingly ordinary to the man who was responsible for calling in an exorcist. James Renick wasn't Catholic, but they were the only church who provided special training for exorcists and something had to be done.

"I don't see why you think the old place needs an exorcism," Father Michael was saying. "I've looked into the history of the place and there's no record of witches living there. There's never been a graveyard on the site, Indian or otherwise. No ley lines cross there. Apart from the story about the young couple who had it built in the 1800s just after the whole street was newly laid, there's no record of a murder on the property."

"That murder was a grizzly mess." Mayor Renick ran his fingers through his short, salt and pepper hair and looked away from the priest. "Thank God they didn't have photographs back then. The very idea of walking into the place and finding such mutilation turns my stomach."

"It's also the sort of thing a sick killer might do. They didn't have the media to report those incidents back then, but there have always been people with disturbances of the mind."

"But it's the sort of thing that has happened in possessed

houses before," Renick stated. He looked sideways at Father Michael, as if he actually hoped for concurrence.

"Exorcism is something we do on possessed people," Father Michael explained. "For houses we do a blessing."

Renick's mouth twisted into a sceptical frown.

"But you will go out and have a look? It seems to me a blessing is pretty low key for some of the stuff I've heard goes on out there around Halloween."

The priest looked down at his hands in his lap, fingers locked together as if some instinct told him there was cause to feel nervous. When he looked up again, his cold, blue-gray eyes held authority.

"Halloween is tomorrow. Keep a watch on the place to keep kids out and I'll go out the day after, All Saints Day. Just in case there's anything to it." Father Michael stood and took a few steps towards the door.

"Wait!" Renick called. "Let me call in Williamson to give you a first hand account. He works here now, but he used to work for the security guard firm we use to watch the place every year and he's got some stories that you ought'a hear."

The priest nodded and returned to his chair while Renick made the internal phone call. The small town civic building only had half a dozen rooms and Williamson entered the office just a few heartbeats later.

He was a tall man, with pale skin and dark, fashionably-styled short hair, but it was the look in his eyes that Father Michael noticed right away. Father Michael could see a haunted quality in Williams' eyes, something the priest had seen rarely in his life. The last time he had observed such an expression, he had still been in seminary and had accompanied a senior priest to a particularly nasty exorcism. The

12

girl's parent's eyes had displayed a similarly disturbed aspect when the priests had first arrived. Father Michael learned soon after that the parents had witnessed some terrifying manifestations from their own child.

There wasn't another chair, so Williamson had no choice but to remain standing. He began twisting his fingers together nervously as soon as Renick explained why he had been called in.

"Father Michael here has agreed to go check out Number 23 Hazelwood Avenue the day after Halloween. I thought he should hear what you have to say about the place and what kind of hijinx this year's security guard might have to be ready for."

"You're sending a guy out there by himself?" Williamson's eyes opened so wide that Father Michael could see the whites of his eyes all the way around the hazel iris.

"Budgets. You know we have to make cuts where we can." Renick shifted uncomfortably in his chair. He found it difficult to make eye contact with Williamson.

"No, you can't!" Williamson pressed his hands on Renick's desk, leaning over him, exuding vehemence. "You've gotta have two guards and they have to stay together and outside of that Hell hole, just to keep kids out. It's not safe!"

Williamson pushed himself off the desk and turned to the priest. Father Michael leaned back as if blown backwards by the man's fervour.

"Father, I'm not Catholic but if your church has any special power over evil spirits, I'm begging you, go out and see the house for yourself. Don't wait until after Halloween! If anyone gets past the security guard..."

"What do you expect to happen?" The priest spoke in

13

tranquil, unruffled tones in an attempt to calm the agitated man.

Renick leaned forward, keeping his words composed and unflustered, following Father Michael's example.

"Why don't you tell the good Father the story you've told every year since you joined the city council, Patrick? And remember, embellishing is just like lying and you don't want to lie to a priest, do you?

"I've never exaggerated anything. I swear, Father, by all that's holy, what I'm going to tell you is absolute truth."

Patrick Williamson paced up and down the floor for a few seconds, his eyes darting in various directions and his hands continually wringing together as he spoke.

"It was a few years ago. Two of us were assigned to watch the place. Me and a guy called Brian Collins. I'd heard the stories but I never believed in ghosts. Know what I mean?"

He stopped and looked at Father Michael. The priest gave him an understanding nod, indicating he should continue.

"We were just supposed to watch the perimeter, make sure no kids got in. Same as every year. It was a nice enough night. Not quite winter, maybe a little late summer even. The moon was pretty bright."

Williamson stopped to gaze out the office window, as if to reassure himself that the world was normal in daylight.

"Collins saw something in an upstairs window. Just a flash of light. We talked about whether some squatters might have got in. We'd just about talked ourselves out of going in to look when we heard a big thump. There was no question, it came from inside."

He spun round, first meeting Renick's eyes, then shifting his gaze back to the priest.

"The minute we went in, everything was just... wrong!"

"How do mean, wrong?" Father Michael leaned forward, interested now. Williamson hesitated, apparently gathering his thoughts before he tried to explain.

"It was like the walls closing in, or stretching in weird directions. Like something you would see in a movie. We got disoriented, had trouble finding our way back out. We didn't care if there was anyone else in there by then, we just wanted out! Then..."

Williamson had paled. He suddenly couldn't seem to make eye contact with either of the other men in the room.

"And then?" Father Michael prompted.

Williamson turned to the priest, his eyes wild with terror.

"Then we heard a deep, reverberating laughter. It actually shook the walls of the room we were in. I..."

Williamson dropped his gaze to the floor.

"I embarrassed myself, couldn't hold my bladder with that demonic chuckle mocking our efforts to escape. We were at its mercy."

"So how did you get out?" Father Michael was rapt with attention now.

"Collins pulled me out," Williamson admitted. He's one of yours, a Catholic. He had a gold crucifix he wore all the time and he'd started praying as soon as things started going weird. Somehow he found the way out and he pulled me along with him. We stayed out in the car for the rest of the night, me praying with him. We only got out of the car if we saw someone getting close to the house. Caught some kids with my high beam flashlight and scared the bejeezus out of them thinking we were cops. Sorry Father!"

Williamson held his palm out as if he could stop the offensive words from reaching the priest's ears. Father Michael, nodded pleasantly, letting the slight blasphemy pass unremarked.

"I quit the security company the next morning. I was never going on an assignment like that again! Father, please say you'll go out there today! Before it's Halloween! If they send a guard out by himself... you could be saving his life!"

"That'll be all, Williamson." Renick tried to communicate his disapproval of putting the priest on the spot with his glare.

"Yes, Mayor Renick," Williamson stammered. "I'll... get back to my desk."

He ducked his head sheepishly and slipped out the door. As soon as it clicked shut, Renick turned to Father Michael.

"So, what do you think? Hallucination maybe? He's assured me many times they weren't drinking."

Father Michael steepled his fingers in front of his lips.

"The mind is a strange thing. If it was just one man... Have you ever spoken to this Collins who was there with him?"

Renick shook his head.

"I tried to look him up when Williamson first told me the story. The security company told me he didn't just quit the next day, he moved out of town. Rumor got back that he joined the priesthood, but I had no way of checking that. Just had to take it at face value and continue keeping people out of that house every Halloween."

"I think I will stop by the house today," Father Michael stated. "Have you got a key?"

"There's no locks on the doors. Never have been."

Father Michael raised his eyebrows at this revelation.

"Surely even people in the 1800s locked their doors?"

"Not this house," Renick insisted. "Might explain how some maniac got in to massacre that young couple."

Father Michael stood up again.

"I'll go have a look, then. And I'll find out about Collins. If he did join the priesthood, that's something I can check myself."

"Can you let me know what you find? Maybe come back tomorrow or give me a ring?"

Father Michael nodded his assurance.

"I saw a budget motel on my way into town. I'll get a room there for a couple nights and let you know how things go, one way or the other."

Chapter Three

By the time school had finished for the day, Tesha had made up her mind. Whatever her friends chose to do, she wanted nothing to do with sneaking out of Amy's party to go creeping around in the house at Number 23 Hazelwood Avenue. Not only would she be betraying her parent's trust, but it would also be putting Amy's parents in a difficult position. They were to be present at Amy's house to make sure the party had some semblance of supervision, but they had promised to be unobtrusive, watching television out of the way in a parlour.

This put their responsibility for a houseful of teenagers in a vulnerable position. The occasional walk-through to be sure no one was sneaking off to the bedrooms or passing drugs or alcohol around was okay for most kids, but someone determined to sneak out looking for trouble elsewhere would find it far too easy. Tesha had decided that person was not going to be herself.

Besides, the old place was all but condemned. Someone could get injured in the derelict house and who among them could do much more than run for help? She and Phillip had taken a basic first aid course together, but that would be of limited value if someone broke a leg or got a serious cut from broken timber on a doorframe or stair banister or something.

Tesha was just about to step off the school grounds when Phillip came running up to her.

"Tesha! Come quick! The twins, Jack and Keith Nash are on the roof throwing firecrackers at Mr. Murphy!"

Phillip grabbed her hand and pulled Tesha towards the elective classrooms before she could protest. Inside her mind she balked. Running towards trouble made no sense. Mr. Murphy was a known tyrant, but if someone got hurt or police were called, the smart thing to do was to not be anywhere near the incident.

Sense didn't come into it as far as Phillip was concerned. Any excitement in this small town was likely to gather a crowd, especially anything to do with the school. As usual, his first thought had been to literally drag his best friend into the fray.

What the strictest math teacher ever known to humankind was doing near the elective classrooms, Tesha couldn't guess. She knew she should be resisting Phillip's impulse to draw her into something that, after all, wasn't her fight. She did well in math class and only occasionally fell foul of Murphy's tendency to torment his students or embarrass those who didn't get the highest grades. The Nash brothers, on the other hand, seemed to be at war with the obnoxious teacher. The twin boys were science whizzes, but too rambunctious to pay attention in a terminally boring math class with Mr. Murphy droning on incessantly about the beauty of higher equations.

Phillip led Tesha around a corner into a crowd of students, jeering equally at the twin brothers and the reviled teacher. Loud pops of firecrackers split the air, with each of the boys taking turns at lighting and throwing one towards a cowering Mr. Murphy. He kept trying to run first one way, then the other off the patch of lawn beneath the classroom roof where the hail of offensive weapons continually dropped to halt his progress, exploding in front of his face in whatever direction he took.

A siren wailed in the distance. The town only possessed two police cruisers, which gave the boys a fifty percent chance of whether they might get arrested by the generally bad-tempered deputy or... the police captain. Their father.

"They're going to be in soooo much trouble!" Tesha turned and saw Ava Davis at her elbow. The younger girl had an amused grin plastered on her face. "They'll miss Amy's party if they're locked up for the weekend."

"They're only sixteen," Phillip reminded her. "They rely on that to stay out of jail."

"They could be grounded, though," Tesha suggested.

"Yeah," Ava mused, dripping sarcasm. "Like last time they were grounded and crawled out Jack's bedroom window to go vandalize Aaron Banks' car for turning them in. I'm betting they at least spend the night in a cell this time. Look!"

Tesha turned to see the police captain approaching from the parking lot. The crowd had already begun dispersing and the Nash twins had disappeared over the other side of the classroom roof, presumably to gain distance and try to concoct a lame alibi somewhere. Mr. Murphy, freed of his ordeal, stomped directly towards the police captain, waving his arms in an animated rant before he was even close enough to be within hearing distance.

"See you tomorrow night!" Ava suddenly ran off towards her brother, Dylan, whom Tesha could see sauntering away with a group of older boys, including Phillip's brother, Raymond.

"Her parents are letting her go to the party?" Tesha scrunched her brows in dismay.

"Dylan will be there to look out for her." Phillip sounded

unconcerned. "And Raymond has a thing for her so she won't be out of our sight."

"That's creepy." Tesha twisted her mouth, looking like she just swallowed a wasp. "Didn't she only just turn fourteen?"

"Yeah," Phillip laughed. "Not to worry though, she doesn't like him. I think she has a crush on Jack Nash, actually. Besides, she'll be jailbait after Raymond's birthday next month. Can you imagine my brother being old enough to vote? Now that's creepy!"

They started to walk back around the corner towards the front exit of the school.

"Sp-speaking of tomorrow night," Tesha stammered. "I've been thinking about it and I don't want to go to 23 Hazelwood. It's not worth the risk."

"Ah, come on!" bellowed Ava, as she, Dylan and Raymond jogged to catch up. "We need more girls!"

"You're in on that too?" Tesha glanced at Dylan. He flashed her an impudent grin.

"We both are. It's just for fun. Everybody knows there's no real ghosts at the old house. The county's just too cheap to fix it up! Hey, we could do a séance!"

"No way you're doing a séance!" Ava's bulging blue eyes almost made Tesha giggle. She looked so much like her brother, with their sandy-blond hair and Nordic features, but sometimes Ava flashed expressions that looked as if she were Dylan's mother rather than his younger sister.

"Too many people going might get noticed," Tesha pointed out.

Raymond gave her one of his derisive sneers.

21

"It's only the five of us. Or maybe four. Joseph didn't want to go. Phillip wants in, don't you?" He looked pointedly at his younger sibling.

Tesha frowned, watching Phillip give his brother a nervous shrug. She could see from Raymond's expression that he didn't really want her to go anyway. That alone nearly made her change her mind, but she was determined to be sensible.

"You won't tell on us, will you Tesha?" Phillip gave her his best puppydog eyes.

Tesha shook her head. She wouldn't get her friend in trouble, no matter how ill-advised the excursion sounded to her. Ava's look of disappointment tore at her heart.

"We need a planning meeting!" Dylan declared. "Those that are going, come with me!"

Phillip looked back and forth between Dylan, beginning to walk away, and Tesha.

"You go ahead," Tesha encouraged Phillip. "I'll see you tomorrow. We're still doing costumes at my house, right?" She gave him a heartening smile, not wanting to hold him back from his fun.

"Of course we are! I'll bring the stage make-up, like we said."

He took a few steps with visible reluctance to follow Dylan.

Raymond began to turn, his arm coming up as if he would put it around Ava's shoulders. He gave Tesha a final glance with a half smile that made the glint in his eye look predatory.

Tesha's breath suddenly started coming in short gasps. She saw Ava's innocent, unwary expression and despite the girl's brother going along with the group, Tesha felt more than a little uncomfortable about the younger girl being the only female in a troop of boys looking for trouble in that house.

"Wait!" Tesha called. "I'm coming too."

Chapter Four

Father Michael drove his black Ford Focus slowly down Hazelwood Avenue, searching the house numbers for the number 23. The car had been new in 2013 and he had taken good care of it, but his investigations required a lot of driving and the wear and tear was beginning to show. The Pope had encouraged the clergy to drive modest cars rather than the newest models, to show humility, so a new one wasn't in his immediate future. The Catholic Church had come under too much criticism in recent years for too much show of wealth, among other things.

By the time he had passed number 29, it was obvious which house was derelict and unoccupied. The overgrown front lawn and general shabby appearance of the dwelling stood out on an otherwise well-kept neighborhood. He spied a group of high schoolers lurking in front of the property as he approached, probably walking home from school, but they moved on as soon as they saw him pulling up.

An Indian girl among them looked at him with guilt written all over her face. The priest would have bet money, if gambling wasn't a sin, that this particular group had some ill-advised adventure in mind for Halloween. Local 'haunted houses' were always a big draw for teenage antics, whether any actual spiritual activity was involved or not. Old houses held more mundane dangers and Father Michael was glad to know that the city posted a guard every

Halloween to keep curious thrill-seekers out.

He parked right in front and got out of the car, watching the backs of the retreating adolescents. The smaller, blonde girl turned and glanced at him, her mouth falling open in shock. Father Michael smiled to himself. The priest cassock often had an effect on casual observers, one way or the other. No doubt in a small town like this, his visit to the house would be popular gossip before the day was through.

Father Michael walked up onto the porch and grasped the front doorknob, but it wouldn't turn. It felt like it was locked. He frowned and scrunched his eyebrows together. He was sure the mayor had said there were no locks on the doors. Could squatters have moved in and installed their own? He walked down a paved path at the side of the house, noting dead rose vines surrounding the windows of the house and an overly high wooden fence on the neighbor's property. It must have been nine feet tall. He stopped and looked at it with curiosity. Were they trying to block out the view of the unsightly property next door?

He continued to the back of the house. Just like in the front, the grass in the back yard was too long and bushes that grew around the perimeter of the property were painfully overgrown and scraggly. He frowned again. Presumably the county kept up *some* maintenance for health and safety's sake, if only to cut the grass once in a while. Wild foxes could have hidden in the now brown grass of overgrown yard and become a danger to local children and pets. He promised himself he would have a word with Mayor Renick about it.

More dead, dried rose bush vines surrounded the back door forming a natural interwoven trellis, but the door itself was clear. Father Michael tried the handle and found it locked, just like the front door. He had never been one to retreat from a challenge. It was why he had passed the qualification to be trained as an exorcist.

25

He walked back to the side of the house where two dirty windows were blessedly free of foliage of any kind. Even the grass that had once tried to grow around the paving blocks had withered and died long since. Careful not to snag his sleeves on the thorns of the dried rose vines, Father Michael pushed the glass of one of the windows upwards. It wouldn't budge. He tried using his thumbs to press upwards on the wood frame. Still no luck. He examined the window construction carefully. There was no sign of a locking mechanism, yet the window stubbornly refused to move.

The priest took a clean handkerchief from his cassock pocket and rubbed at the dirt on one of the windows to try to peer inside. The dirt was apparently both inside and outside, as he could make out very little through the obscuring filth, even through the portion he had rubbed clean. He stood back for a moment, regarding the uncooperative windows. Painted shut? Wood frames swollen from damp? He contemplated every possible logical explanation.

Father Michael returned to the back of the house. He tried the windows on either side of the back door. Just like the side windows, they were grimy inside and out, though he was able to determine that at least one of them led to a kitchen. And just like the side windows, there was no sign of a locking mechanism, yet the windows were clamped shut, refusing to move even a little.

The priest examined the doorknob carefully. There was no hole for a key. No sign of a lock anywhere, yet it still wouldn't turn. He was down to his last resort now. Father Michael took a vial from his pocket. He stopped to cross himself and mutter a prayer. Then he unstoppered the bottle, threw some of the holy water within onto the immovable door and used his strongest voice of command.

"IN THE NAME OF JESUS CHRIST OUR SAVIOR, I COMMAND YOU TO OPEN AND ALLOW ME ENTRY!"

The door and windows flew open. The previously sunny day

was instantly obscured by black clouds and violent winds. The screams of a thousand voices in torment blasted from within the now opened house, knocking Father Michael down backwards from the force of sound and fury suddenly unleashed. The priest shuddered under the onslaught. An eternal moment later, the screams and the wind diminished, then stopped. The sun shone again. The house stood docile, as if nothing had happened, yet the doors and windows remained open.

Father Michael wondered if the other residents on the street had witnessed any of it. Had the phenomena actually occurred, or had it been a demon-induced hallucination just for his own benefit? He made a mental note to stop by the house next door and ask if they had heard anything. First, he had further business with Number 23 itself.

He got up from the ground, rubbing his tailbone. Father Michael had fallen hard and expected he would soon have a large bruise to show for it. With some trepidation, he stepped towards the open back door. The moment he crossed the threshold, the voices started again, but at a subdued volume. Father Michael had only taken one step fully inside the kitchen when a thick, red ooze that looked like blood started dripping down from the tops of the kitchen cabinets in large gobbets. He recoiled, unsure whether the sing-song moans, like a discordant chorus, had increased in volume a little in response to his repulsed reaction.

One deep-throated moan wailed out forcefully above the rest, accompanied by the shape of a tormented face forming in the wood grain of one of the cabinet doors. It was too distorted to tell whether it was male or female, or even if it was entirely human.

Abruptly, the room seemed to tilt, then distend so that the top part of the room stretched in the opposite direction as the floor. The priest stumbled, disoriented and unsure of his balance. Somewhere in the cacophony of barely audible voices he thought he

27

heard one of them hiss the name, Francis, his secular name before he had taken the cloth.

Father Michael had seen and heard enough. He backed out of the house, closing the door behind him. Just as he heard the click of the latch, both back windows slammed shut with a bang that made the startled priest jump. He quickly stepped further into the back yard, putting distance between himself and the house, taking short, gasping breaths. He forced himself to breathe deeply.

He started to lift his handkerchief to his forehead to wipe the sweat dripping into his eyes, then thought better of rubbing the filth of the windows still on the soiled cloth against his skin and used his sleeve instead. He put his hands on his knees to let his blood circulate to his brain to dispel the dizziness, but he couldn't bring himself to duck his head down as he had been taught. He needed to keep an eye on the old house every moment that he was on the property.

Eventually when he got his breath under control, Father Michael slipped down the side path, keeping as much distance from the offensive house as possible, nearly scraping up against the neighbor's fence. He started to walk towards his car, then remembered his intention to query the residents next door. He looked at his watch and discovered that it had stopped. The second hand of the old analog model wasn't moving. Father Michael turned and ambled up to the refreshingly ordinary house and rapped on the door.

A few more deep breaths later, a woman answered. She gave the impression of an ordinary housewife; a slight woman with short, brown hair wearing mint green polyester stretch pants and a yellow top that looked like it came from Kmart. She looked him up and down curiously.

"Sorry to bother you," he apologized. "But I wondered if you've heard anything from the house next door today?" He indicated which side with a nod of his head. A look of alarm came over the woman's features.

"Number twenty-three?" Her voice went up an octave as the words tumbled out. Father Michael nodded in the affirmative. The woman looked in the direction of the house next door, then she looked back over her shoulder into her own house and stepped outside, closing the door quietly behind her. She turned back to the priest.

"I haven't heard anything today. Sorry Father."

"But you've heard something from there before?" Father Michael could read people well. Exorcist training included some psychological tuition, to learn to differentiate between someone with a mental illness and a person who was actually possessed.

The woman spoke in a low voice, obviously avoiding being heard by someone inside the house.

"We moved here a little over seven years ago. The realtor told me no one lived over there, but that the county maintained the property. From what I've seen they don't maintain it very well! Anyway, I wandered over one day, just curious. Like anyone would. A window was open at the side of the house and I was afraid it was left open accidentally and the rain might get in, so I reached up to close it. Well, of course I took a peek inside."

The woman's eyes shifted left and right and she started wringing her hands together.

"Go on," Father Michael encouraged her. "I've heard some strange stories in my time. You won't shock me and I won't dismiss anything you say. Promise."

He gave her his most reassuring smile. Suddenly she looked up into his eyes, fear emanating from her every pore.

"A voice called to me. It used a name I haven't heard since I was a child, sort of a family nickname. Everyone who ever knew that name is long since dead!"

Father Michael used his most soothing manner to calm her down.

"It's alright Mrs...."

"Smith," she supplied. "Margery Smith. The nickname was Marja. My grandmother was Finnish."

"You've stayed away from the house ever since?"

"I had that fence built to keep it out of my sight! I won't even walk that direction without crossing the road. That voice was creepy... sinister! Father, are you going to get rid of... whatever is in that house? I can't sell this one or we would have moved away years ago!"

"That's what I'm here for," he assured her. "The church is aware of the problem now and we have trained specialists to deal with any eventuality. Thank you for your candid information, you've been very helpful."

Father Michael kept his heartening smile in place long enough to turn around and walk to his car. As soon as he was inside the vehicle with the partial privacy of reflective windows, his face dropped. He was trained to perform exorcisms on possessed people. The house was something unprecedented in his experience. He opened the glove compartment and took out a cell phone, then dialed a number he knew as well as his own.

"Your Excellency, I've been to the house. I'm going to need back-up."

Chapter Five

Tesha preened in the mirror, appreciating the artistically curved whiskers Phillip had drawn on her face with his stage make-up. Sometimes it paid to have a friend in drama class. Phillip had participated in every school play since they had started high school as freshmen, either as cast or crew. He had aspirations towards professional theater after graduation and Tesha hoped her friend would achieve success in his ambitions, though she would miss him if he moved to New York.

"What do you think, Phillip, not too clingy?" Tesha indicated the black jumpsuit she wore for her black cat costume. A body-hugging costume would never pass her mother's inspection, but this was passable as street wear and the fake fur tail she had attached could be easily removed. Add a headband with cat ears, painted whiskers and a little extra eyeliner, plus watercolor painted claws on a pair of black boots that would wash off, and the costume was complete.

Phillip, of course, had gone whole hog and dressed up in an elaborate Captain Jack Sparrow costume authentic enough to challenge the professional impersonators, though his features didn't resemble Johnny Depp at all. Still, all the girls thought he was cute and Tesha had to admit he made a great pirate, if perhaps a little baby-faced.

"I think you'll pass," Phillip agreed. "Then you can tighten the belt before we get to Amy's." A wink that would come over as flirtatious on anyone else signified that her best friend was only teasing.

Just then, Tesha's ten-year-old sister, Aarya, wandered into the open door of her room, wearing a shiny satin lion costume bought from the supermarket.

"So, are you guys going to the haunted house tonight?" Tesha's smile dropped and she locked eyes with Phillip for a split second before answering.

"What haunted house? We're going to a Halloween party at Amy's."

"Oh come on," Aarya groaned. "Everybody goes to 23 Hazelwood on Halloween. I went there last year with Emma and Chloe. It was awesome!"

Tesha spun around at Aarya's admission.

"What happened? You didn't go in, did you?"

"Nah." Aarya plopped herself down on Tesha's neatly made bed. "We got as far as the porch and the door creaked open, really slow like in the movies! There were some weird noises inside. I figure someone was playing a joke. Then a security guard came around the corner and chased us off."

"Could have been some perve," Phillip admonished. "Good thing you *didn't* go in! There could be transients holing up in abandoned houses like that."

"Or maybe it was ghosts or voodoo spirits!" Aarya opened her eyes wide and mimicked someone telling a scary story, wiggling her fingers towards the teenagers.

"What kind of weird noises?" Tesha's expression nearly made Aarya laugh. She looked just like their mother when she was getting ready to disapprove of something.

"Like someone hissing and singing, calling me. They called me Aggie, so I figured you had to be in on it somehow. No one else ever called me that."

"And I haven't since you were four." Not for the first time, Tesha began to doubt the wisdom of the excursion planned for that night.

"Just stay away from there," Tesha reprimanded her sister. "If Mama found out, you'd be grounded for life."

Aarya rolled her eyes dismissively.

"Are you going trick-or-treating tonight?" Phillip asked, intentionally diverting the conversation.

"Yep," Aarya answered in a clipped voice. "Chloe's mother is shadowing this year."

Tesha smiled at her sister's term for a parent walking a few paces behind children who thought they were too old to have their mother accompany them trick-or-treating, but still young enough to have protection nearby. Aarya and her two school friends had trick-or-treated together since they first started school, their mothers taking turns accompanying the small group of girls.

The doorbell rang and Aarya suddenly bounced out of the room.

"There they are!"

Phillip and Tesha exchanged a knowing smile.

"Such innocence," Phillip mused.

"We should be on our way too," Tesha reminded him. "If we hurry we can slip out in the chaos of getting the kids on their way before my mother has a chance to give me 'the lecture'."

"Let's go!" Phillip agreed. Tesha checked to make sure she had everything she needed and they tramped down the stairs, while Tesha shouted to her busied mother that they were off to Amy's house now and she would see her in the morning. Her mother opened her mouth as if she would say something, but her hands were occupied straightening Aarya's lion's mane and in the end, she settled for wiggling a few fingers by way of waving goodbye.

A short walk later, they found Raymond, Dylan and Ava waiting outside Amy's house. Ava looked cute in her witch costume. Dylan and Raymond had made minimal effort by wearing old, scuffed jeans and torn shirts and smearing dirt on their cheeks, presumably dressed as tramps. As planned, Phillip and Tesha had arrived 'fashionably late' by about twenty minutes to give more people time to show up. There was safety in numbers and in getting lost in a crowd.

"About time," Raymond scolded. "I was beginning to think you two chickened out.

"Relax, Raymond," his brother admonished. "We can't show up with just a few people here and then disappear. Have Amy's parents seen you?"

"Yep," Ava chirped. "We were some of the first arrivals! Got all the best cookies too!"

"Good." Tesha peered through the open front door, observing the increasing population. "I think Phillip and I should make a point of being seen. Besides, it's polite to at least say hello to Amy. Enjoy the party for a while before we sneak out."

"So when and where do we meet?" Dylan asked.

Tesha looked from one face to another, wondering if anyone had been listening during their planning meeting.

"Let's give it an hour. Walk around as much as possible so anyone there will remember seeing each of us. Then about ten o'clock we all wander out to the gazebo in the back yard. The fence behind there is low and we can climb over to the alley behind the house pretty easily."

Tesha was amazed at how confident she sounded, as if she planned illicit excursions all the time. Inside, her guts were churning at the thought of what would happen if they got caught.

As soon as everyone had agreed to the plan, Tesha went inside on her own, to be followed by Phillip after a short interval. Raymond, Dylan and Ava stuck together as a unit, ostensibly to look after Ava as Dylan had promised his parents he wouldn't be separated from her for a moment because she was too young to be left to her own devices at an all-nighter.

Tesha followed her own advice, spreading herself around and talking to as many people as possible. As luck would have it, Amy's father happened into the kitchen just when she was helping herself to a can of cream soda from the supply provided for the party. She chatted to him briefly, then wandered out and 'accidentally' ran into Phillip. They even danced together when the random music generator played *The Monster Mash*.

Luckily Phillip had a watch and was able to furtively alert Tesha when it was nearly ten o'clock. They wandered out to the back yard, trusting to shadows and the disinterest of a few other party goers outside to make their way to the gazebo without drawing undue attention. There was no sign of the others yet.

They found a place to sit on the far side of the gazebo that would keep them out of sight of any casual glances. Tesha wondered if anyone would think there was something going on between her and Phillip, but it couldn't be helped. School gossip could be brutal.

After a few minutes, Raymond sauntered out of the darkness, closely followed by Dylan and Ava. Tesha used hand signals to direct everyone to the low spot in the fence and one by one, they climbed over. It was just a little too high for Ava, but Dylan lifted her and allowed Raymond to help pull her over. They walked as quietly as they could to the end of the alley and turned right, towards Hazelwood Avenue. The escape had gone as smoothly as clockwork.

Number 23 Hazelwood Avenue presented a new challenge. Everyone knew there were security guards posted there every Halloween. Thanks to Raymond's friend, Joseph, they knew there would be only one this year, but a single security guard was enough to put an end to their adventure.

Ava, because she was small, volunteered to creep up and see if she could find out where the guard was. Chances were that he would sit in his car all night, if not fall asleep in it. If she was seen, she could pretend that she was just out trick-or-treating.

"Besides," she argued. "My lucky amulet will protect me." She held up a large, oval amulet she wore around her neck as part of her witch costume. The rounded stone with the hole in the middle reflected the dim street lights, despite its dark surface.

"Where did you get that?" Dylan asked.

"From Aunt Laurie." Ava gave him a smug smile.

"Oh, well, it really is magic then. Aunt Laurie's the whacko of the family." Dylan's derisive tone piqued Tesha's curiosity.

"What makes her a whacko?"

Dylan smirked, but turned his head as if admitting his family weirdness embarrassed him.

"She really believes all that magic stuff. Keeps candles and crystals around her place and all that."

"Maybe there's something to it?" Tesha suggested.

Once again, Phillip stepped in to get things back on track.

"Ava's the smallest and the only one that looks young enough to get away with saying she's just a trick-or-treater. If she stuffs her blonde hair up under her hat and keeps the brim shadowing her face so it doesn't reflect the light, she might not get seen. I say we keep her in sight, but let her run recon."

He turned to Dylan. Ava's older brother nodded.

"Ava, you don't go in that house alone. You just look and tell us what you can see."

"Don't worry," she promised. "I won't forget you guys waiting out here and make you miss all the fun." She stuffed her hair into her hat as Phillip had suggested, pulled the brim down to shadow her face, then skulked off into the darkness. The street lights provided some illumination and Tesha was able to follow the younger girl's progress most of the way, but then Ava disappeared into a shadow and Tesha lost sight of her. The group stood quietly, waiting for their spy to return. Tesha wondered if Dylan felt as uncomfortable about his sister ducking out of sight as she did, but she didn't want to ask.

The minutes stretched by like hours. Nobody spoke, but the boys started to fidget. Tesha was just about to suggest they go look for Ava when the girl's pale face suddenly appeared out of the darkness.

"Boo!"

Dylan was the only one who jumped. Tesha speculated that he had probably been the most tense of them all because he was supposed to be responsible for his sister's safety.

"So what did you see?" Raymond asked.

"Not a lot," Ava reported. "I think the car out front belongs to the guard, but there's no one in it. I walked around the whole perimeter and didn't see anybody. He might have gone inside."

"They don't usually go inside," Phillip murmured.

"If he's inside he'll have to use a flashlight. We can see him before he sees us." Tesha looked from one face to another, seeing her nervousness reflected in the others' expressions.

"Unless he sees our flashlights first," Raymond reasoned. "Or are you suggesting we go in without them?" Raymond looked at Tesha as if she had made an incredibly stupid suggestion.

"I didn't say that!" she defended herself quickly. "We just look first, before we turn them on. Keep them pointed down before we go around corners and stuff."

"Makes sense to me," Phillip said quickly. "Let's go."

"And we stick together from now on," Dylan insisted. "No more separations!"

Ava looked at her brother with open derision and muttered under her breath.

"Baby..."

They moved through shadows as stealthily as they could, all too aware that any excuse they could come up with if they were caught now would sound feeble and unconvincing. Every year, someone tried to sneak into Number 23 Hazelwood Avenue and every year, the security patrol stopped them and sent them on their way. One of the council members had suggested they start making arrests for trespassing, but as the perpetrators were usually good-natured kids. The idea had fizzled quickly.

Each of the group stayed alert, searching every possible shadow or potential hiding place for a guard waiting to stop them. Tesha hoped one would jump out and give her friends a scare, so that they had no choice but to return to Amy's party. However, somehow they got all the way to the front porch without incident. There was still no sign of a security guard and Tesha wondered if the man had gone down to the cafe or something, neglecting his duty.

A tense moment passed with all of them standing on the porch, waiting for someone else to take a step forward and reach for the door knob. Then slowly, with an almighty rusty creak, the door swung open by itself. The teenagers all looked at their friends' faces, eyes opened wide, except Dylan.

"This is a set-up, isn't it? Someone rigged the door."

"Or maybe the house settled and it's off balance," Raymond offered.

Tesha rubbed the goosebumps on her arms under her sleeves.

"Interesting timing," she commented. She strained to see inside the darkened doorway, looking for a trap. A smart security guard could have set the whole thing up to catch out trespassers. It's hard to deny intent with your foot inside the door.

"Come on," Dylan encouraged the group, then he strode forward through the opened door. He stopped just inside, then when nothing happened, he turned on his flashlight, keeping it directed at the floor at first.

Ava broke the deadlock first, skipping inside after her brother, then Raymond followed, not to be outdone by a little girl. Phillip and Tesha trailed closely behind him. No one besides Dylan turned on their flashlights yet. Tesha thought to close the door behind them, then Dylan brought up his beam, panning it across the walls to see what could be seen. It was a powerful light, one he used when camping with his father.

"It's just an old house," he stated. The scepticism in his voice calmed some of the tension the others had built up, more from fear of discovery than expectation of encountering ghostly happenings in the old house. Tesha once again began to feel the whole excursion was stupid, not because of the dangers but because Dylan was right. It was only an old house.

The musty smell suggested no one had made an effort to clean inside, ever. Tesha frowned in disgust. Despite the fact that no one had lived there for over a century, the county was supposed to keep the place up, at least a little. She turned on her flashlight and began inspecting the old, flowered wallpaper, looking for mold more than anything else.

The furniture was of an antique style, with carved detail in the wood. The fabrics of the sofa and chair had probably been expensive in its time, but was likely to be rotted now. The very air had an oily feeling to it. Tesha didn't want to touch anything and warned Ava that there could be bugs living in the upholstery. Colors were difficult to tell in the limited light, but looked generally muted, as well as faded.

There were no ornaments on the elaborately carved mantelpiece, but a sizeable painting with a thick, carved wood frame hung above it, showing a nature scene with woods and rabbits leaping through the foliage. Tesha wondered if it might be valuable. The frame itself must be worth a fortune! It looked as if it might be taller than herself and was nearly as wide as the entire mantelpiece.

"This way," Raymond whispered, waving his hand towards an open door to what looked like another large room. He had his light on now and the others followed, except Phillip. He stopped to look at the painting Tesha had discovered. She had just stepped through the doorway to the next room when they all heard a humongous crash. Tesha backed out of the room and directed her light towards where Phillip had been standing under the painting.

"Phillip!" she screeched in panic. Tesha rushed towards the massive painting, growing more agitated as she flashed her light on the thick wood of the frame and imagined what the weight of it might have done to injure her friend. She searched for any sign of him under the edge that hit the floor, but the small relief of not seeing bleeding legs beneath it did little to assuage her fears.

Then she heard a cough from the other side of the painting.

"I'm alright!" Phillip's weak voice called from the other side of the canvas. "I ducked into the fireplace."

Suddenly Raymond was there, helping Tesha lean the heavy frame away from the wall enough so that Phillip could crawl out from his sooty sanctuary. It took their combined strength to move the weighty painting enough for even Phillip's skinny body to squirm out. Apart from a couple more coughs and some smudges on his face and costume, Phillip appeared to be unharmed.

"Shine a light up there, would you Tesha?" Phillip indicated the wall where the painting had hung. Tesha finished helping Raymond lean the painting back against the mantelpiece and shone her flashlight up the wall as requested. Phillip climbed up onto the mantelpiece like a monkey and balanced on the narrow shelf while he examined the hooks that should have held the painting in place. He pulled on them, testing for weakness.

"These are solid," he reported with some confusion in his

voice. "That painting must have hung there for decades. Why would it fall now?"

"Because you were there," Ava intoned in a spooky, singsong voice. Everyone turned to her and she shone her flashlight upwards from beneath her chin while making a strangulated face.

"Very funny," Dylan sneered at his little sister. "He could have been seriously hurt!"

"That's what I was saying yesterday," Tesha ventured. "This place is probably full of hazards. We should go."

Raymond's face twisted, showing his mixed feelings between an adventure barely begun and the very real danger from the close call his brother had just evaded.

"Okay, but in a minute," he prevaricated. "I just saw something that looked like writing on the wall in that other room and I wanted to get a better look at it. We'll go right after that."

Everyone agreed. They stuck close together and returned to the second room, all flashlights on full now. Collectively they spilled enough light around the walls to see nearly as well as in daylight.

Again, the furniture looked very old, but of a quality no longer seen. A hefty oak dining table that would seat eight people stood just to the left of the entrance and was surrounded with carved wood chairs in a style Tesha assumed was Victorian, with embroidered tapestry cushions on the seats and backs.

The walls had no decoration besides the dark red, flocked wall covering itself, but something appeared to be missing from next to the right hand wall. A large, rectangular space where the flooring looked darker than the rest of the room suggested that a heavy piece of furniture had been taken away at some time. Two doorways broke the expanse of the back wall, an open doorway to the left and one with a shut door to the right, presumably leading to other rooms. Tesha thought she could see hanging pans glinting in the darkness through the left hand doorway.

Raymond walked straight to the far wall where some writing had been smeared across the otherwise empty breadth. The letters were only a little darker than the wall covering and several light beams were required to read it clearly. The top line, in letters about eight inches tall, read, "You are lost" and beneath it in letters at least twice the size was a single word, "Forever!"

"I've had enough of this," Phillip declared. "Let's get out of here." Everyone murmured assent and each member of the group moved close to the others and followed Phillip back through the doorway they had just entered through. Even Raymond didn't argue.

To their surprise, the room they stepped into wasn't the same one they had stepped out of just moments ago. There was no front door to take them to the outside. There were no windows. The room appeared to be another sitting room or parlour, decorated in a 1920s style with lighter colors, very different from the room that had been there before. An elaborate chandelier that also had not been there before hung in the middle of the room, lighting the space with burning candles, and the only other doorway was an open arch at the far end.

The teenagers stood with their mouths agape, gazing around at pale gold walls and cherry bent wood chairs with ivory brocade seat cushions, the center of the room empty as if it were meant for dancing. Tesha could still detect the musty smell, but now it was laced with melted wax from the candles. Suddenly some old time music started playing from an unseen source. It sounded like a circus calliope, slightly off-key and playing a Jazz Dance tune.

Ava was the first to break through the group's collective speechlessness to state the obvious.

"I think we're in trouble."

Chapter Six

Father Michael scowled as he drove past several children in costumes. One group of girls was accompanied by an adult woman who stood back while the kids went up onto a porch to ring the doorbell for trick-or-treat. The practice had pagan origins and the church disapproved, but even Catholic children still indulged in the custom, not wanting to miss out on all the fun.

The priest pulled up in front of Number 23 Hazelwood Avenue, just behind an old Chevy. He glanced around for any sign of the expected security guard, but there was no one to be seen. Father Michael got out of his car and walked over to the Chevy, peering inside the dirty windows on the assumption that the car must belong to the night watchman. There could be no other reason for it to be there.

Satisfied that no one was asleep or playing games with a smart phone inside, he went back to his own vehicle to await instructions from the Bishop. Father Michael hadn't wanted to approach the house on Halloween night. Having established that some form of evil dwelt there, it could only be at its strongest on that night of the year. The Bishop, however, had insisted that the town needed protecting and that there couldn't be any delay. He had promised to send help.

Father Michael ruminated on the phone call he had received

from the Bishop that morning. Tracing the ex-security guard who had left town after a night at the property had been fairly easy. Brian Collins had indeed applied to the priesthood. He had gained a minor grade and requested sequestering. Eventually he had been assigned to a retreat center in California.

Gaining his co-operation or gleaning information, however, had proved impossible. Even a direct command from the Bishop to return to the Midwest to help with tonight's business had met with direct refusal. Brother Timothy, as he now fashioned himself, had said he would face excommunication before he would confront the malevolence of Number 23 Hazelwood Avenue again.

Father Michael understood. Despite his training as an exorcist, a house that bleeds like a special effect out of a Horror movie would be enough to send even an atheist screaming for religious protection. He looked at the uncharacteristic shaking of his hands resting on the steering wheel of his car, and didn't mind admitting that whatever foul spirit possessed that house was beyond any training or experience he could call on. The Bishop, however, had known a priest who had encountered malicious house entities before. Father Joshua was on his way now, driving down from a diocese in Indiana.

The journey was estimated to take approximately five hours. Father Joshua had left just after four o'clock in the afternoon, so could arrive at any moment. Father Michael wondered if the priest would be in adequate shape for the task ahead after a long, no doubt exhausting drive. Like Father Michael, Father Joshua was a trained exorcist. Father Michael hoped that the senior priest's experience would make up for his own doubts concerning the situation. Not every exorcism worked the first time. Father Michael feared they might be facing a very powerful spirit this night.

He sat in the delusive safety of his own car, preferring boredom over tackling the malevolent presence on his own. He was prepared to spend the entire night waiting if necessary. Morning would dawn onto All Soul's Day, a much more auspicious time to tangle with the supernatural. Nearly an hour passed, during which many children in costumes passed by the darkened house on their trick-or-treat rounds. The neighboring houses had their porch lights on, indicating that they had candy ready to dole out. Only one other house on the street besides Number 23 was dark. Just across the road and one down, a house with neatly trimmed hedges effectively barricading the front yard showed no welcoming porch light for the trick-or-treaters. Whether the inhabitants disapproved or just couldn't be bothered to provide candy, Father Michael didn't know, but the house was obviously occupied and the property well-maintained.

The children appeared to get older as time dragged on and quickly became less frequent after about nine-thirty. The porch lights turned off, one by one, until the street was lit only by the yellowish glow of street lights. Father Michael had just begun to worry about what might have delayed Father Joshua, when his cell phone rang.

"Hello? Father Michael speaking."

"Hello, Father Michael, this is Father Joshua. I've had a slight delay. I'm sorry to keep you waiting."

"Is everything alright? We can leave this until morning. I'd actually prefer it." Father Michael mouthed a silent prayer, hoping Father Joshua would agree.

"It's just a little fender bender on the freeway," Father Joshua explained. "No one was hurt and the car still runs fine, but we've had to exchange details and talk to the police. You know how these things are."

Father Michael nodded, then remembered that Father Joshua couldn't see him over the phone. He had never been in even a minor car accident himself, but he was aware of the necessary procedures.

"Yes, I'm familiar with the legalities. But we don't want to be doing this at midnight..."

"That's why I want you to go ahead and start without me."

Father Michael felt his stomach drop. He opened his mouth to respond, but Father Joshua was already talking.

"In my experience, malevolent house spirits are usually discarnate souls. Performing a House Clearance is very similar to an exorcism of a possessed person with very slight adaptations. Do you have holy water with you?"

"Yes Father, I brought a large bottle. I wasn't sure how much we would need."

"Did you bless it yourself?"

"Yes Father."

"Standard blessing?"

"Yes Father."

There was silence for a moment, then Father Joshua asked a question that surprised Father Michael.

"Are you familiar with the Rite from the Roman ritual for blessing water with salt?"

"I've... heard of it, but I've never..."

"I'm going to text you a transcript. While you're waiting for me, I'd like you to get some salt somewhere and bless the salt first, then the water all over again, using the blessed salt. All the instructions will be in my text."

Father Michael hesitated a heartbeat before answering.

"Yes, Father Joshua. Whatever you think is best."

"When you've completed the rite, you can start the prayers for exorcism, but whatever you do, don't go inside the house. This is important. Repeat it back to me."

Father Michael felt a twinge of irritation at having to repeat instructions like a child, but it was his place to obey a senior priest.

"I will do the blessing of salt and water, following your instructions exactly, then I will begin the prayers for exorcism, but I will not set foot inside the house."

"Good," Father Joshua acknowledged. "I should be there in about half an hour. Repeat the prayers if you have to, but wait for me before proceeding further."

"Yes, Father. I will certainly wait for you."

"See you in about half an hour," Father Joshua finished, then he hung up, not waiting for a response.

House Clearance, not House Blessing, Father Michael thought. The subtle difference in language made all the difference in meaning. Father Michael wished he had known the right term when he had spoken to the mayor. He vowed he would remember it when he delivered a report to the man later.

As much as he would rather have performed the blessing rite in a church, the hour was getting late and he had his instructions. Father Michael leaned over to open the glove compartment of his car. He kept it neat and stocked with only those things that he deemed practical; insurance papers, ice scraper, SatNav, road maps and a small plastic box where he kept packets of salt, pepper and ketchup from fast food restaurants in case he had to eat in transit. It felt less than sacred to take out a packet of ordinary salt for his purpose, but the blessing to come was intended to make the

49

difference.

He heard the tone from his phone that indicated a text received and sat up to read Father Joshua's instructions. It included many (+) marks to indicate that he should cross himself during the ritual. It felt awkward to perform the rite sitting in a car and not standing over an Altar, but there was little choice. The trick-or-treaters had thinned out until none were left by then, so he need not feel self-conscious about bystanders observing the ritual.

The rite was written for at least two people to perform, but he was on his own and would have to read both parts. Father Michael quieted his mind as he took out the bottle of holy water he had blessed before, then he began:

"Our help is in the name of the Lord. Who made heaven and earth."

He picked up the salt packet and tore it open.

"O salt, creature of God, I exorcise you by the living (+) God, by the true (+) God, by the holy (+) God, by the God who ordered you to be poured into the water by Elisha the prophet, so that its life-giving powers might be restored. I exorcise you so that you may become a means of salvation for believers, that you may bring health of soul and body to all who make use of you, and that you may put to flight and drive away from the places where you are sprinkled; every apparition, villainy, turn of devilish deceit, and every unclean spirit; adjured by him who will come to judge the living and the dead and the world by fire. Amen."

Father Michael lowered his head in prayer.

"Almighty and everlasting God, we humbly implore you, in your immeasurable kindness and love, to bless (+) this salt which you created and gave to the use of mankind, so that it may become a source of health for the minds and bodies of all who make use of it.

May it rid whatever it touches or sprinkles of all uncleanness, and protect it from every assault of evil spirits. Through Christ our Lord. Amen."

He then opened the holy water bottle and held it up as best he could in the cramped conditions, offering it to God.

"O water, creature of God, I exorcise you in the name of God the Father (+) Almighty, and in the name of Jesus (+) Christ His Son, our Lord, and in the power of the Holy (+) Spirit. I exorcise you so that you may put to flight all the power of the enemy, and be able to root out and supplant that enemy with his apostate angels, through the power of our Lord Jesus Christ, who will come to judge the living and the dead and the world by fire. Amen."

Again, he lowered his head to pray.

"O God, for the salvation of mankind, you built your greatest mysteries on this substance, water. In your kindness, hear our prayers and pour down the power of your blessing (+) into this element, made ready for many kinds of purifications. May this, your creature, become an agent of divine grace in the service of your mysteries, to drive away evil spirits and dispel sickness, so that everything in the homes and other buildings of the faithful that is sprinkled with this water, may be rid of all uncleanness and freed from every harm. Let no breath of infection and no disease-bearing air remain in these places. May the wiles of the lurking enemy prove of no avail. Let whatever might menace the safety and peace of those who live here be put to flight by the sprinkling of this water, so that the health obtained by calling upon your holy name, may be made secure against all attack. Through Christ our Lord. Amen."

The incongruity of the standard litany to his specific circumstances brought a moment of doubt to Father Michael. No one lived in the house. No one had lived there for more than a century. It was unlikely anyone ever would live there, but the rite had its formula and to deviate would be more risky than to try to interpret it to fit his needs. Father Michael slowly poured the salt into the bottle in the form of a cross, as the instructions indicated.

"May a mixture of salt and water now be made, in the name of the Father, and of the (+) Son, and of the Holy Spirit. Amen. The Lord be with you. And with your spirit."

He wasn't sure who this part could be directed towards, since he was doing the rite alone, but it was in the text and therefore must be included. For the third time, he lowered his head and prayed aloud.

"O God, Creator unconquerable, invincible King, Victor ever-glorious, you hold in check the forces bent on dominating us. You overcome the cruelty of the raging enemy, and in your power you beat down the wicked foe. Humbly and fearfully do we pray to you, O Lord, and we ask you to look with favor on this salt and water which you created. Shine on it with the light of your kindness. Sanctify it by the dew of your love, so that, through the invocation of your holy name, wherever this water and salt is sprinkled, it may turn aside every attack of the unclean spirit, and dispel the terrors of the poisonous serpent. And wherever we may be, make the Holy Spirit present to us, who now implore your mercy. Through Christ our Lord. Amen."

With the salted holy water prepared, Father Michael had no excuse to procrastinate further. He looked at the clock on the car dashboard. Only ten minutes had passed since his call from Father Joshua. In theory he should arrive in twenty minutes, but driving times were never precise. The least he should do is begin the prayers for exorcism as Father Joshua had instructed.

He opened the car door and got out, then grabbed the car roof as his knees buckled under him. A fluttering feeling in his stomach turned to light nausea and he wiped a drop of sweat dripping from his forehead into his eye with the back of his shaking hand. Father Michael stopped to count how many exorcisms he had attended in his career as a priest. He had assisted at three, but he had never performed one on his own. A primal terror threatened to take over his thoughts when he gazed up at the darkened upper floor windows of the house at Number 23 Hazelwood Avenue.

Father Michael took several deep breaths, calming himself. Warnings about the deception of the enemy played through his mind. He told himself that his fears were illusion, created by the malevolence within the house. It had, after all, capitulated entry under the power of holy water the previous day.

He pulled his shoulders down to stretch his tensed neck muscles. It was an old trick, actually learned in a public speaking course for dispelling stage fright nerves, but it was effective. Father Michael took one more deep breath and strode purposefully up to the front porch.

Steeling himself against any residual fears, Father Michael began the litany in English and threw a light sprinkling of holy water onto the front porch.

"Lord have mercy. Christ have mercy. Lord have mercy. Christ hear us..."

Suddenly there was a thunderous roaring sound and the front door flew open. Father Michael took a step backwards in surprise, then stepped up onto the porch, stopping at the threshold of the door.

Whatever you do, don't go inside the house.

Father Michael stood his ground, refusing to enter the dwelling at whatever invitation the open door implied. The street lights shone just enough light through the door to make out the shapes of furniture, as if he were looking inside an ordinary room. He began again.

"Lord have mercy. Christ have mercy. Lord have mercy. Ch-Christ hear us..."

He trailed off, spellbound by some kind of movement he could only just detect on the back wall of the room, near a doorway. Father Michael squinted his eyes, trying to determine the shape of something that appeared to separate itself from the wall, black against the darkness of a patterned expanse in shadow. Slowly, the shape took form and Father Michael felt the blood leave his face. A pair of enormous, bat-like wings flapped into the room with a voluble whoosh of hot air.

Despite his terror, Father Michael strained to see what sort of creature would form between the wings to confront him. He held up the bottle of holy water and splashed some towards the entity, suddenly noticing that somehow he had entered the room. He had no sooner realized his mistake when all light blinked out, leaving him in total darkness.

Chapter Seven

Dylan turned to look through the doorway they had just come through. The dining room was still visible, but without the illumination of the living room windows, everything looked considerably dimmer.

"What do we do now?" He scratched his head, screwing up his expression like a kid in a 1950s wholesome sitcom.

"We stay together, like you said." Raymond was the eldest among them and it felt only natural for him to take charge. "Nobody goes in any other rooms without the group. We don't want to get split up."

"There have to be doors to the outside and windows somewhere," Tesha suggested logically. "We've just got turned around somehow."

"Except this room is too big for a house on this street," Phillip observed. "It's almost big enough to call it a ballroom."

Tesha frowned at Phillip's assessment. He was right.

Without warning, a burst of warm air blew through the room like a desert wind, rattling the chandelier and blowing over an ornate, embroidered chair. The teenagers instinctively ducked and pressed against a wall together. Then suddenly it was gone and the room was just as before.

"Well," Ava declared. "*That* had to come from somewhere!" She marched across the room to the open archway on the far side of the room.

"No, Ava, don't go through!" Phillip called. Ava stopped right at the threshold, put her fists on her hips, and looked from side to side at whatever was on the other side of the doorway. The others stumbled towards her, afraid that she might step through despite the warning.

"I'm not stupid, you know." Ava's sarcasm received a smirk from her brother. "We only just now said we should stay together! I do know a thing or two about magic and that room changed. It could happen again."

"What do you know about magic?" Dylan jeered.

"Aunt Laurie tells me things. And I read books. That's why she gave me the amulet." Ava held up the black, oval amulet she had worn with her witch costume.

"Maybe you should try using that amulet to find us a door to the outside so we can get out of this place," Raymond suggested. It was hard to tell whether he was indulging the younger girl or just mocking her. Ava gave him an odd look and clutched the stone in her hand.

"This is silly." Phillip craned his neck to look through the arched doorway. A hallway lined with old fashioned oil paintings was dimly lit by an oil lamp sitting on an old telephone table from another era. Closed wooden doors at either end blocked sight of what rooms the hallway led to, but the entrance from the room they still stood within opened onto the middle of the corridor, giving them an even choice of which way they could go if they proceeded through.

Tesha tucked the tail of her cat costume into her belt. Between the candles on the chandelier and the oil lamp, there were far too many open flames around to have part of her costume hanging loose. The thought that bothered her most, though, was who had lit them.

The Calliope music behind them suddenly seemed to become louder and further off-key. The group turned and saw ghostly dancers in the middle of the room they had just crossed, stepping and spinning in dance moves that were completely at odds with the style of music. They appeared to be dressed and moving in a manor that would suit Mozart rather than Jazz.

"I'm scared now," Ava whispered to her brother.

"I think we all are," Dylan hissed back.

As if in silent consensus, all of them stepped into the dimly lit hallway, preferring the eerie atmosphere to openly sharing a room with ghostly figures. Again, Raymond took charge.

"Come on, this way." He led them off to the right, stepping quickly at first, but he had to slow down when the others shuffled more slowly, gazing at the paintings on the walls with their eyes opened wide in trepidation.

Tesha wondered if it was only her own imagination that made it look as if the eyes on the people in the paintings followed her movements. She knew that some paintings could produce that illusion if the eyes were painted a certain way. She held Phillip's hand, comforted by his reassuring presence. Dylan and Ava also huddled close together in sibling solidarity, though they didn't hold hands. Raymond stayed a step ahead of the group, trying his best to get them to move faster without speaking. Somehow the echo of their own voices in this place felt wrong.

When they got to the door, the others caught up to Raymond

one by one. All of them looked from one face to another in their group, even Raymond. Making the decision to open a door to the unknown suddenly implied a tremendous responsibility. After a moment, it was Dylan who took a deep breath and reached for the doorknob. He turned it slowly, then opened the door as if he expected something to jump out from within. Inside was complete darkness.

"Let's get some light in here, where's all the flashlights?" Tesha scrunched her eyebrows in a pained expression as she lifted her flashlight and turned it on. How had they all forgotten about them? Phillip and Raymond also turned on their lights, each thinking to themselves that it was odd they had no memory of turning them off.

Dylan led the way, relying on the light beams from the others to illuminate the room they entered. Ava stopped for a moment to struggle with hers as it was a little heavy for her and it had got tangled in the draping fabric of her witch's robe pocket. After a moment she got it loose and turned on the beam. She walked through the door only a split second after the others, but the room was dark, with only her own flashlight offering any relief from the enclosing darkness. There was no sign of her brother or their friends in the room.

Ava scanned the room as best she could with a single flashlight beam. It appeared to be some sort of large storeroom with shelves and glass jars, which thankfully appeared to be empty. The smell was musty at best, and perhaps a little rancid as if a rodent had died and left the odour of decomposition to blend with the general reek of dust and decay.

The light shook a little. Ava quickly worked out that it was her own hand that was shaking the flashlight. Despite the smell, she took several deep breaths, attempting to calm herself from the shock of suddenly finding herself alone. Normally she was happy to be by herself. Ava preferred reading books to going out to parties and she only had a few friends. Amy's party had been an exception because the older kids were going. Most kids her age were too immature and she preferred her brother's friends over kids in her own class.

There were no other doors in the room she had entered. With no alternative choice available, she stepped back out of the door to the hallway that led to the ghostly ballroom. The music still played on, but Ava let out a breath of relief that at least the hallway was the same as before.

This still left her with only two choices. She could try to retrace the route the group had followed through the house. This would mean crossing the parlour, or ballroom, whatever it was meant to be. Regardless, the music suggested the dancers would still be there. She couldn't be certain that they would ignore her passing. There were far too many of them to take the risk.

That left the door at the other end of the hallway. Like the one she had just returned through, it might lead to anywhere. She took a couple of steps down the hallway, keeping as quiet as she could, then she turned and tried the door to the storeroom again. She opened it carefully, watching for any surprises, but when she shone her light inside, it was the same as before.

She let out a sigh and turned towards the other door. She would have to pass the open doorway and the ghostly dancers to get to it. Ava put away her flashlight and crept along the hall, silent in her light, canvas shoes that she had worn with her costume. When she got to the hallway, she peeked around, showing as little of herself as possible.

The dance continued. The dancers concerned with their revelry took no notice of the small girl in her witch costume. Ava kept her eye on them as she all but tip-toed past the doorway. When she got to the middle of the open space, one of the dancers turned and stared at her. It was a woman in eighteenth century dress, white and pale, until their eyes met. Then the dancer's eyes turned red and began to elongate. She hissed at Ava and a long, forked tongue rolled from her open mouth, fangs forming like a giant cobra.

Ava ran the rest of the way to the end of the hall, praying that the entity, whatever it was, wouldn't follow. In her imagination, she saw the ribboned dress forming scales and the woman transforming into a snake to slither after her. The hairs on the back of her neck raised and Ava felt a tingle all over her body. Her breaths came in sharp gasps as she came to the door.

She clutched the amulet her aunt had given her and muttered under her breath.

"Take me to a room where I can get out of this house!"

There was no time for rhymes or spells, not that she knew how to perform such a thing. She beseeched the stone directly, trusting to whatever magic it held to help her when no other aid was to be found. She opened the door, forgetting her flashlight until she saw the dim light within, then hearing that sinister hiss drawing nearer, she shuffled through and closed the door behind her.

She took out her flashlight and quickly inspected the room. It was a bedroom with an old-fashioned four poster bed in one corner and a standing carved wooden wardrobe that was probably worth a fortune in antique value. The dim light had come from the two windows on the opposite wall. Ava hurried over to one of the windows and looked outside. Somehow she had got into an upstairs bedroom. The view looked over the back yard of the house next door. Despite the night time shadows, the normality of the scene was comforting.

Ava had no idea how she had ended up upstairs when she

hadn't climbed any steps, but she wasn't going to go through any more doors, now that she had a glimpse of the outside world. She pushed the window open and looked for a way down that wouldn't break her neck. She decided then and there that when she got home, *if* she got home, she would demand one of those fire escape ladders made of rope that hooked on a window sill for her own bedroom.

A large oak tree in the neighboring yard had a branch overhanging the stupidly high fence. It had been a few years since Ava had done any tree climbing, but she was pretty sure that if she could launch herself far enough to land on a thick part of that branch, she would be able to climb down. The skirts of her costume might present a problem, but there was no one around. She could hike it up and stuff it into her underwear, though her legs would probably get scratched up.

The tricky part was making the jump. The branch wasn't far below the window, maybe four feet, but there was a distance between the window and a substantial part of it that might hold her weight, perhaps a three foot leap. The smaller branches that would just break off reached fairly close, creating an illusion of safety where her good sense told her it wasn't very safe at all. However, going back through the bedroom door and looking for a stairway, then trying to find her way out of the house again just wasn't going to happen. There was no choice. She had to jump.

"Where's Ava?" Dylan had his flashlight out now and turned towards the tail end of the proceeding group.

"She was just here," Raymond mumbled. He opened the door

to the hallway, wondering who had closed it and when, since he had been the last to come through. There was no sign of the girl, only the creepy music echoing down the hall. "She's not here."

"I have to find my sister!" Dylan insisted. He stepped towards the door.

"We can't split up!" Raymond countered. "We'll all end up separated and lost forever! We can get some help and come back for her."

"You don't get it!" Dylan looked miserable. "I can't go home without her. I'm responsible for keeping her safe!"

Tesha laid a comforting hand on his arm.

"Raymond's right. Ava is a sensible girl. She's in no more danger than the rest of us, but you're right too. We need to find her. We just need to stay together to do it. We should try to work out where she could have gone."

They used their flashlights to look around the room they had entered. Tesha's was beginning to lose power. The room looked like a Victorian man's private study, with a heavy oak desk and high-backed oak chair. Shelves of books lined one wall. Phillip panned his light beam across the books, reading titles that spanned law, science and geography. The books were old and covered with dust, probably outdated in their content by at least a century, though the bookbinding art was very much in evidence.

Like the other rooms, there were no windows. This one had no door apart from the one they had entered through. Dylan, visibly agitated, began circling the room, knocking on walls and examining details the others could only guess at.

"There's no other way out," Raymond capitulated. "We should all go look for Ava."

Everyone agreed, but when Raymond tried to open the door again, the doorknob wouldn't turn. It was as if it were locked, though there was no keyhole.

"It's stuck!" he gasped in surprise. At that moment, the room began to shake like an earthquake. A loud, deep rumble drowned out any further exclamations and seemed to echo around the room in a circle. Books fell off the shelves and an ink bottle and pen fell from the oak desk. Tesha thought she heard a deep-toned laugh somewhere within the rumble, the sound cloaked among the crashing and roar of the unexpected phenomena.

When it stopped, Tesha, Phillip and Raymond were clutching whatever piece of furniture they found nearest to them. Their eyes had opened wide in panic and their faces paled, but now that the disconcerting tremor had halted, they began to breathe again.

"Where's Dylan?" Phillip asked, first to notice the boy was missing from their company.

"He can't have gone anywhere," Raymond reasoned. "The door was closed the whole time and there aren't any others!"

The three of them looked around the dishevelled room. Tesha noticed one bookcase slightly askew and walked over to examine it.

"Look!" she called to the others. "There's some kind of passageway behind here!"

Raymond was still closest to the door and tried the handle one more time. It wouldn't budge.

"Well, I guess that's where we go now. Maybe Dylan went that way. I don't know where else he could have gone."

"Or maybe he fell through," Tesha warned. "Let's get our lights in here and look out for anything like a hole in the floor or trap door. Let's not take any chances."

The three of them proceeded cautiously, examining the walls and floor with their flashlights at every step. The passage they stepped into was narrow and devoid of decoration or light, apart from what they provided for themselves. The darkness swallowed the beams, rendering even Tesha's high-powered light inadequate.

A strange hiss sounded to their left. All three flashlights turned their beams towards the strange noise. Tesha felt her mouth drop open at what looked like the body of an enormous snake slithering along the wall, then her light sputtered out. Raymond and Phillip kept their flashlights trained on the moving shape.

"Is it a snake?" Tesha's voice had taken on a shrill note, even in a whisper.

"It's gotta be at least a foot wide," Phillip speculated with something like awe in his tone. "I haven't seen anything like that outside of a zoo!"

"Where did it go?" Raymond took a step closer to where they had seen the movement, but that was as far as he would go.

Phillip shone his beam around the room, straining to see in the impeded light.

"I don't see it. I don't see anything."

A loud crack followed by the groan of strained wood over their heads diverted their attention to the ceiling. The light beams snapped up, illuminating a protruding fissure progressing across the ceiling as if something heavy were about to fall through on their heads. Raymond, Phillip and Tesha instinctively threw themselves against a wall. At the same moment, the flashlights went dark and they were left in complete blackness. Tesha let out an ear-splitting scream that pierced the night.

Chapter Eight

Father Michael took a deep breath and almost choked on a sulphuric stench. He closed his eyes. He was trained for this. He would not allow himself to panic. He lifted the bottle of holy water over his head and spilled a little, allowing it to trickle over his hair, face and cassock. He took a tentative step backwards in the darkness. Logic told him that if he had somehow fallen into entrancement and stepped forward, stepping backward now should take him back through the front door. Two more steps later, his progress was halted by a solid surface.

He felt around the wall behind him, first one direction then the other. There was no indication of a door of any kind. Keeping his head, he began to sprinkle holy water around the perimeter of the room while saying aloud the Prayer to St. Michael the Archangel, continually feeling for doorframes or window sills.

"IN THE NAME OF THE FATHER, AND OF THE SON, AND OF THE HOLY GHOST. AMEN. MOST GLORIOUS PRINCE OF THE HEAVENLY ARMIES, SAINT MICHAEL THE ARCHANGEL, DEFEND US IN OUR BATTLE AGAINST PRINCIPALITIES AND POWERS, AGAINST THE RULERS OF THIS WORLD OF DARKNESS, AGAINST THE SPIRITS OF WICKEDNESS IN THE HIGH PLACES."

Father Michael had no doubt of what he was facing now. Father Joshua's theory that it would be no more than a discarnate soul had clearly been wrong in this case. The disgusting odour, the leathery wings, the ability to somehow change the layout of the room... he was in the presence of the enemy himself, or one of his more powerful demons.

"COME TO THE ASSISTANCE OF MEN WHOM GOD HAS CREATED TO HIS LIKENESS AND WHOM HE HAS REDEEMED AT A GREAT PRICE FROM THE TYRANNY OF THE DEVIL. HOLY CHURCH VENERATES THEE AS HER GUARDIAN AND PROTECTOR; TO THEE, THE LORD HAS ENTRUSTED THE SOULS OF THE REDEEMED TO BE LED INTO HEAVEN. PRAY THEREFORE THE GOD OF PEACE TO CRUSH SATAN BENEATH OUR FEET, THAT HE MAY NO LONGER RETAIN MEN CAPTIVE AND DO INJURY TO THE CHURCH."

Father Michael opened his eyes and continued his litany, alert for any response from the entity. Though he was blind in the complete darkness, he could sense its presence in the room with him. The air itself felt congealed, like a pervasive, cloying miasma of pure evil.

"OFFER OUR PRAYERS TO THE MOST HIGH, THAT WITHOUT DELAY THEY MAY DRAW HIS MERCY DOWN UPON US; TAKE HOLD OF THE DRAGON, THE OLD SERPENT, WHICH IS THE DEVIL AND SATAN, BIND HIM AND CAST HIM INTO THE BOTTOMLESS PIT, THAT HE MAY NO LONGER SEDUCE THE NATIONS."

Suddenly two points of light became visible in the pitch darkness. They glowed an eerie red as if tail lights of a car had reflected into the room, then they took shape and Father Michael found himself staring directly into the gaze of a pair of red, glowing eyes with slanted pupils. He faltered a little, breaking his formula.

"Get thee behind me Satan!"

The eyes shut, leaving him in total darkness again. Then behind him, Father Michael heard a deep, menacing chuckle. The direction of the menacing sound reverberated around the walls of the room, as if the enemy surrounded the lone priest. For the first time in his career as an exorcist, Father Michael felt his knees quake in stark terror.

✑

Ava wedged her feet against the window sill, hoping she could spring far enough across the expanse before gravity took over. She only had to manage a six foot jump to get to a thick part of the branch. Just a foot more than her own height. A fall from second storey height was certainly good for a broken bone or two. However, she was fairly sure it wouldn't be fatal. Either way, she had to try.

She had seen the gymnastics girls fling themselves further than the distance between her and the branch. Sure, they practiced all the time and had the muscle tone, but the necessity of escape drove Ava onward. Having stuffed the skirt of her robe out of harm's way, she felt rather exposed and vulnerable. Her whole body trembled with fear of failure. It would have been easier if there had been a soft lawn beneath the window, but a paved path awaited an unsuccessful attempt, promising pain and probable injury.

There was no help for it. Ava had to try, whatever the consequences. She closed her eyes and took a deep breath, then let it out slowly. She took another deep breath and opened her eyes, focusing on the part of the branch she wanted to reach.

Think like a frog, think like a frog!

She remembered things her aunt had told her about observing the animal world and learning from them. A frog could jump far. So could she. Ava wiped sweat from her forehead, surprised to find it there on a chilly night. She wiped her hand on the cloth of her robe quickly and tensed up, ready to make her leap. High and far, like a frog...

She tried to push off, but her body refused to obey on the first try, nearly making her slip off the window sill. She took two rapid deep breaths, pushing the air out on the first one, then on the second exhale she shut down her mind to every thought except the leap. She sprang upwards and outwards, then plummeted towards the ground sooner than she ever would have expected.

A part of the branch far too thin came within reach and she grabbed it in panic despite knowing it couldn't possibly hold her weight. The branch bent with her descent, then to her amazement, her foot caught on something, scraping her ankle but arresting her fall. Ava found herself precariously balanced between the inadequate branch and the top of the fence, where her foot had caught. With part of her weight supported by the fence, the branch proved strong enough to hold the rest, for the moment.

She clutched the branch for dear life, breathing heavily and gathering her thoughts to decide what to do. The fence was sheer wood without climbing holds. It was too high to jump off. The tree branch felt flexible and she was now suspended over the soft lawn of the house next door, though this time of year the ground could be deceptively hard. She could call for help, perhaps get the attention of the people in the house. That would mean getting discovered with her robe skirt stuffed in her underwear and her whole lower body exposed.

With her arms growing tired and her ankle stinging, she decided she couldn't wait for rescue and the subsequent embarrassment. She grabbed the branch as tightly as she could and pushed off the fence.

Again, she plummeted towards the earth, but this time the yielding branch slowed her drop until she was only four feet from the ground. There was a sudden loud crack and Ava landed sharply on the lawn, discovering every jagged rock hidden within the grass. She looked up at the lighted windows of the house to see if anyone might have heard the branch snap and come running out.

Apparently the television she could hear blasting some old movie had covered the noise. She turned and looked up at what she could see of Number 23. Dark windows were just visible above the fence. For just the blink of an eye, she thought she saw a glimmer of light pass across the window she had climbed through to make her escape, then it was gone. She couldn't be sure whether she had imagined it.

Ava got up slowly, checking herself over for any sign of injury. Her ankle was bleeding, but it was just a scrape. She pulled the robe out of her underwear and smoothed the fabric down, making herself fit to be seen. Then she crept out to the street, ducking under windows where the people in the house whose yard she had borrowed might see her.

Once out front, she could see the front of Number 23 Hazelwood Avenue clearly again. It looked much as it always had, except there were two cars parked on the street in front of the house. There was no sign of flashlights in the windows, though she knew her brother and friends had some with them. Ava ran over to the parked cars, hoping the missing security guard had returned to his because she needed to tell someone about the kids still trapped inside, but who? Her parents couldn't do anything. All that would do was get all of them in trouble for leaving the party.

There was no one inside the Chevy, just like before. She looked at the other car, a black Ford Focus with a decorative mother of pearl cross hanging from the rear view mirror. Then she remembered the priest they had seen pull up to the house yesterday. Could this be his car? It looked the same. But where was the priest? Ava turned and looked at the house again, remembering the disorienting experience she and her friends had experienced inside. Could a priest be captured the same way?

Ava absentmindedly reached for the amulet at her throat, then noticed what she had done. The amulet had helped her find a way out. Ava was sure of it. Her Aunt Laurie's house was just a few blocks from here. She took off running in the direction of her aunt's house. Aunt Laurie would know what to do. Ava turned at the corner just as a pair of car headlights came around the same corner, heading down Hazelwood Avenue. Ava couldn't see the car very well from just the street lighting, but she didn't recognize it. She put it out of her mind, assuming it was one of the people who lived in one of the normal houses on Hazelwood Avenue.

Father Joshua saw a young girl wearing a witch costume running on the sidewalk as he turned the corner of Hazelwood Avenue. He frowned, disapproving of the costume but concerned what the girl might have to run from. He didn't see any pursuers. She hadn't been screaming for help and his current business was urgent, so he left her to her own business.

Finding the address didn't prove difficult. Every house on the street looked well-kept with recently mowed front lawns, except one. Father Joshua pulled up behind the black Ford Focus already parked in front of the house. Another car was also parked in front of it. It looked as though Number 23 was the most popular house on the street that night.

Father Joshua got out of his car and looked through the windows of the other cars. There was no one inside either, but an ornate crucifix hung from the center mirror of the Ford. He guessed that one probably belonged to the priest he had come to meet, Father Michael. But why wasn't he in the car, waiting, since there was no sign of him in front of the house? His instructions had been to begin the rite, but not to go inside.

Father Joshua turned and startled as a black cat on the pavement behind him hissed at him, curving its back up in a classic Halloween cat pose. The cat then darted away and Father Joshua took a few deep breaths to steady his heartbeat. He looked harder now that his eyes had had a moment to adjust, but still saw no sign of anyone on the front porch. Father Joshua frowned, considering the possibilities of what might have happened to Father Michael.

As a precaution, he followed the side path by the house to the back, to see if Father Michael might be approaching the house from the greater privacy of the back yard. The priest was nowhere to be seen. Father Joshua tried the back door. The knob refused to turn, as if it were locked. He had been told the house had no locks on the doors or windows.

He stood back and regarded the house. A flicker of light drew his attention to an upstairs window, which appeared to be open. Father Joshua cocked his head, perplexed by the anomaly. Surely no one would be inside? Except perhaps Father Michael, if whatever entity caused the strange happenings at the house might have tricked him inside in some manner. Father Joshua could think of no other possibility. A qualified exorcist would not abandon his post. With the priest's car still parked out front, there could be no other explanation.

Father Joshua returned to his own car and retrieved a bottle from the glove compartment. He had dealt with too many

71

supernatural entities of various natures to depend on another priest, no matter how competent, to be solely responsible for making sure they would have enough holy water. He had brought a large bottle of his own, properly blessed with salt.

He returned to the front porch, but was not surprised to find the front door of the house locked to him, just like the back door. Something didn't want him inside. The malevolence he could sense emanating from the house had a familiar tinge to it. His assumption that it would be just another discarnate soul left a taste of dry ash in his mouth. He had sent Father Michael in unprepared. Even before any phenomena began to show itself, Father Joshua could sense that this was something stronger.

Chapter Nine

The ceiling continued to crack, forming a bulge nearly a foot thick before the plaster began to fall in chunks. It began to look as if the entire structure would come down. Phillip and Tesha shrieked in desperation, pushing themselves up against the wall behind them and feeling around in hopes of finding another secret door.

Raymond kept his head. He meticulously felt along the length of the dimly lit wall for any sign of an opening. There was still no clue about where Dylan had gone. A deep, thunderous rumble came from the fissure as if several floors above were caving in with only seconds before the weight of it all would fall on their heads. At last Raymond found a straight indentation and shoved what he hoped was a door with his shoulder. It opened, allowing a flickering, yellowish light to spill into the crumbling passage.

Phillip and Tesha ran towards the escape, not caring for the moment where this new door would lead them. The three of them tumbled into the strangely lit room and Raymond pulled the door shut behind them. All sounds stopped. One by one, each of them turned to examine the room they had come to this time, wary of what hazards might await them next.

The door they had come through looked like an ordinary wooden door, albeit with an elaborate design carved into the wood. The round, brass knob gleamed in the dim light. Raymond tried to turn it carefully, confused by the cessation of sound from the hallway they had escaped. It refused to budge. Pulling and rattling the doorknob did no good.

The rest of the room appeared to be some sort of workroom. A large, oak table dominated the center of the space, but there were no chairs. It was set high, as if used as a workbench. Low shelves surrounded the walls, filled with a haphazard array of metal tools and rolls of what looked like leather. Unusually straight, wood poles leaned up against one corner. The ceiling was high and what light was available came from a window at least eight feet above the floor on one slanted wall, suggesting it led to the roof.

"A window!" Tesha exclaimed. "We can get out!"

"How do we get up to it?" Phillip examined the articles in the room, seeking anything that might be of use.

Everyone was silent for a moment, then Raymond came up with an idea.

"The table! If we can lean it up against the wall, I can climb up."

"Or fall and break your neck," Phillip challenged. "Maybe if we unroll some of these skins, one will be big enough to drape over halfway to use it like a rope."

"It would have to be a full cow hide," Tesha cautioned.

Raymond sneered at her practicality.

"So let's unroll some of the bigger ones and see what we've got."

Tesha refused to acknowledge Raymond's usual obstinacy and pulled what looked like a large roll of leather from the shelf. Phillip helped her roll it out on the table, but it didn't cover it all the way.

"I could jump up if we find something a little bigger," Raymond suggested. He turned and pulled another roll from a shelf. Tesha, not wanting to risk any accidental physical contact with Phillip's insufferable brother, took a different one from a shelf and started to unroll it on the floor. She watched from the corner of her eye as Phillip helped Raymond unroll what appeared to be a good-sized cow hide and didn't observe what her own bundle revealed until it was nearly fully displayed. Tesha had to acknowledge that hers wasn't nearly big enough for their purpose. She looked down at it and let out a piercing shriek.

"What is it? What's happened?" Phillip was by her side in the blink of an eye. He looked down at what Tesha had laid out on the floor and started to hyperventilate, pulling her away.

"I don't want to touch it to roll it back up!" Tesha insisted. Phillip looked as if he might vomit over the grisly revelation.

Raymond, despite the irritation displayed by his furrowed brows, gave in to curiosity and walked over to see what all the fuss was about. He looked at the skin displayed on the floor, grotesquely lit by the shaft of light gleaming through the high window, and felt his stomach convulse. The empty skin was undeniably human.

"Come away," he said, suddenly sympathetic. "Let's just get out of here. We can tell the cops about this later."

The others didn't argue. Phillip and Tesha followed Raymond back to the worktable, now draped with the massive skin Raymond had found. The color was difficult to determine in the half light, but there was no pattern. To Tesha's eyes it looked like a dull gray, as if somehow the creepy workroom had access to dinosaur skin.

"Is it strong enough?" Tesha gingerly tried pulling the edge, still wondering what sort of creature the skin might have come from. It seemed too thin to be cowhide or to hold Raymond's weight. He was as tall as a man already and muscular, unlike his more bookish brother.

"I'm up for a try." Raymond looked up at the window, then back at the table. If we drape it halfway and you two get under the table and hold onto one end so it doesn't slip, I can probably get up fast enough to keep much pressure from pulling on the... leather." He had nearly used the word 'skin', but decided against it after their gruesome discovery.

"What if the table slips down and crushes us?" Phillip, always the optimist, gave his brother an impish grin.

"The legs will stop it, doofus. And if I slip, I'll just slide down. We've done crazier stuff than this enough times."

Phillip had to agree. How they had got as old as they were without breaking more bones, or worse, had been a mystery since he got old enough to stop following his brother onto the roof of their house and up all the neighborhood trees. Raymond could climb like a monkey and Phillip had followed his brother's lead for years, until a fall from an apple tree had resulted in a broken arm for Raymond when Phillip was ten and Raymond eleven. The next day, Phillip came home to see his brother swinging by his cast from a branch of the same tree. That was when he decided he would be the more cautious brother, though he was still a better than decent climber.

"Okay let's do it," Phillip said. They each grabbed onto the end of the table and tried to push. Nothing moved.

"It's really heavy," Tesha grumbled, immediately hoping Raymond wouldn't mock her for the redundant statement.

"Good, solid oak," he acknowledged instead. "You just don't find furniture like this anymore. We'll have to use leverage."

"How?" Phillip leaned on the table in defeat. Raymond,

however, refused to be beaten.

"We tip it over on the long side, then while it's balancing on the edge, push so the end gets as close to the window as we can get it." Raymond pointed as he spoke, using his hands to try to draw pictures in the air.

"Just make sure the legs are facing the wall," Phillip insisted. "I don't want to get crushed to death!"

It took all of their strength, but the three of them were able to get the table moving over towards its long side, then Raymond shifted it to lean on a corner before it settled so that it balanced. From there it was easy to turn it the way they wanted. Tesha remembered part way into the procedure to pull the animal skin over the edge that would be at the top so that it hung partly down beneath the table. The part still on the table top covered just slightly over half the length of the table.

As soon as the makeshift ramp was settled into place and Raymond had tested it to see that it felt secure, Phillip and Tesha crouched underneath and took hold of their end of the leather skin. The window was still a few feet higher than the edge of the table, but nobody questioned Raymond's ability to make the final leap.

"Okay, hold it tight!"

Tesha responded to the sound of Raymond's voice by grabbing the end of the skin and holding it as hard as she could. Phillip did the same next to her. They heard Raymond's feet echo on the floor as he ran across the room, then leapt up onto the table like a Parkour champion. Tesha and Phillip could tell he was pulling himself up by the edge of the leather from the proximity of his grunts, yet it didn't pull on their end. The weight of the table with Raymond on it held the skin in place against the wall securely.

They heard his feet shuffle on the edge of the table, then a final grunt as he pulled himself up by the window ledge. Luckily the ledge beneath the window was wide enough that a slim boy could perch on it for several minutes if necessary.

"I'm up!" Raymond called down to them. Then a moment later, "It's locked. I'm just going to see if I can work it out!"

"How will we get up when he gets the window open?" Tesha whispered to Phillip.

"We can make it," her friend assured her. "One good run will get you far enough to grab the skin, then we can pull you up if we have to."

"What about the other side? We don't know what kind of drop is out there."

"We'll work it out." Phillip had never been one to give up on a challenge. "There's always a way, we just have to find it. Even if it's shouting at the neighbors to call out the fire department."

Tesha laughed nervously, thinking about the scene that would ensue if her parents had to come to a rescue situation.

"Tesha," Phillip murmured in an even softer voice. "We've been best friends since we were six. There's something I have to tell somebody, but I don't want Raymond to know."

"You know you can tell me anything." Tesha's imagination went into overdrive, wondering what her best friend might have to confess in a harrowing moment of stress.

"This is important. You have to promise you won't say anything in front of my brother. I just don't want to die without telling someone and you're the one person I feel I can trust completely." The earnest look in Phillips eyes reflected in the dim light. Tesha could see that whatever he had to say was something very serious to him.

"You're not going to die!" Tesha gave him a forced exasperated look. "Raymond will get the window open and we'll get out of here and get some help to find out what happened to Dylan and Ava!"

"We may all die trying to get out of here. But promise me!" Phillip's vehemence convinced Tesha that it was something important.

"Pinkie swear!" she promised, trying to lighten the mood. Phillip hesitated for another moment. Tesha dreaded the possibility that he might confess that he had feelings for her beyond friendship that would turn their friendship awkward. To her, he had always been like a brother.

"The reason I never asked you out..." Phillip took a deep breath and lowered his voice so far Tesha had to strain to hear. "Tesha, I like boys."

"You mean you're gay?"

"Shh! He'll hear you!" Phillip flicked a glance upward to indicate Raymond. They could hear a series of scrapes and rattles from his attempts to open the window.

"You're coming out to me when we're about to die?" Tesha's voice sounded incredulous.

"You just said we aren't gonna die!"

"It doesn't sound like Raymond's having much luck."

"We'll get out. Just promise me, Tesha. Don't say anything to Raymond. He might tell my father and Dad would disown me!"

Tesha nodded her agreement, but she wanted to encourage her friend. Nobody should have to hide who they are from their own family.

"Maybe he won't be stupid about it."

"You've heard how Raymond talks. You're gay if you do this, you're gay if you think that. Always in derogatory terms."

"A lot of people talk that way." Tesha saw how stupid the statement was as soon as the words were out of her mouth. "Most of them don't mean it, not when it's real."

"I can't afford to lose my brother. If he turns on me, if he tells my dad..."

"You think your dad won't understand?"

"I know he'll react badly," Phillip contended. "He goes all funny when my mom's gay brother visits for Christmas."

"You know what they say about people who react badly to gay people. They usually harbour gay tendencies themselves."

"Are you saying my dad's gay?"

Tesha wondered how much further she could put her foot in her mouth.

"No but... just don't let it worry you so much. I understand why you're scared to tell your family, but you've told me now and it makes no difference to me. You're my best friend and always have been. I'll support you through whatever."

Phillip turned and hugged her, just as they heard Raymond sliding down the table in front of them.

"It's no good," he reported. "Whatever's holding that window in place isn't budging."

Phillip's face clouded over with anger. The stress of the situation made something inside him snap.

"Then we'll have to budge the window itself," he raged. "It's made of glass and this room is full of metal tools."

Phillip stomped over to one of the shelves on the opposite side of the room and rummaged through the apparently random selection of implements until he found two that he was satisfied would serve his purpose. Tesha and Raymond drifted towards him, trying to work out what it was that he planned to do. They had just got close enough to see a long, heavy chisel in his hand and a hammer in the other when Phillip turned, glaring at the offending window.

"Phillip, no," Raymond entreated. "Let me do it."

Determined to prove he could be as useful as his older brother, Phillip ignored him and sprinted towards the table.

"At least let us hold it steady!" Tesha called after him.

Phillip got no chance to answer. A loud rumble shook the house and just as Phillip reached the middle of the floor, the entire center of the room collapsed and a red, glowing radiance shot up, illuminating the room from unknown depths. Phillip plunged, screaming, into the abyss, followed by the table and the human skin they had left unregarded on the floor.

This time Tesha's screech came from the bottom of her diaphragm.

"Philliiiiip!" She lunged, as if she would catch him, but he was too far away. Raymond grabbed her by the waist, stopping her from throwing herself after her friend into the seething, crimson froth of what looked like magma within the still forming pit. The edge of the floor continued to crumble, moving closer to them.

Tesha screamed Phillip's name over and over, struggling against Raymond's restraining arm, then she collapsed in tears, shaking her head as if her denial would somehow bring him back.

"Phillip's gone," Raymond murmured in Tesha's ear. She turned her head and saw his jaw set and moisture in his eyes as he tried to pull her away. It was Raymond's loss too.

The floor continued to fall apart, the edge drawing nearer by the second. The window was unobtainable now. The only entrance was the door they had come through to escape the disintegrating hallway. Raymond tried the doorknob with his free hand. It turned.

"Turn on your flashlight," he commanded, transferring his arm from Tesha's waist to a hand holding her arm to tow her after him. He pulled the door open and Tesha pointed her failing flashlight beam into the darkness. There was no rubble from the previous fragmentation of the ceiling. The passage looked as if nothing had happened. With no other choice and the crumbling edge of the floor behind them getting closer, Raymond dragged Tesha into the darkness and closed the door.

Chapter Ten

Father Joshua splashed a little holy water onto the front door of the house, then stood back in the middle of what would have been the front lawn if the county had kept up maintenance on the property. The long grass streaked the hems of his cassock with evening dew. The priest was, however, more concerned with what else might find a convenient hiding place in the all too adequate ground cover. This part of the country wasn't known for poisonous snakes, but if his suspicions about the house were accurate, vile creatures of diverse sorts might well have become attracted to the malevolent energy emanating from a spiritual viper's pit.

As he had done in the back yard, he stood regarding the house for a few moments, observing the upstairs windows as well as those downstairs. For just a blink of an eye, something that looked like a reflection of red light flashed across all of the windows from right to left. The other houses on the street showed no such reflection.

He took a deep breath and let it out slowly, then Father Joshua began the rite of exorcism, murmuring it softly at first.

"In the Name of Jesus Christ, our God and Lord, strengthened by the intercession of the Immaculate Virgin Mary, Mother of God, of Blessed Michael the Archangel, of the Blessed

Apostles Peter and Paul and all the Saints, and powerful in the holy authority of our ministry, we confidently undertake to repulse the attacks and deceits of the devil."

The house let out a reverberating groan, as if the wood it was made of spoke aloud. Father Joshua began to quote from Psalm 67.

May God be gracious to us and bless us

and make his face shine on us

so that your ways may be known on earth,

your salvation among all nations.

The windows snapped open all at once and blood-red light shone out as if a comet glowed from the core of the structure. A refrain of many voices moaning that sounded like a cacophony of cries of the damned echoed from within the crimson light. Father Joshua began shouting the words of the exorcism rite, struggling to make them heard over the chorus of voices.

"WE DRIVE YOU FROM US, WHOEVER YOU MAY BE, UNCLEAN SPIRITS, ALL SATANIC POWERS, ALL INFERNAL INVADERS, ALL WICKED LEGIONS, ASSEMBLIES AND SECTS. IN THE NAME AND BY THE POWER OF OUR LORD JESUS CHRIST, MAY YOU BE SNATCHED AWAY AND DRIVEN FROM THE CHURCH OF GOD AND FROM THE SOULS MADE TO THE IMAGE AND LIKENESS OF GOD AND REDEEMED BY THE PRECIOUS BLOOD OF THE DIVINE LAMB!"

Twice he crossed himself as the voices grew louder. Father Joshua continued the litany, crossing himself repeatedly at appropriate points in the rite that he knew well. The red light slowly dimmed and the voices began to fade. When he came to the end of the prescribed ritual, the house stood dark and silent. Father Joshua strode up onto the porch and tried the door again, wetting his hand first with holy water. It clicked open.

He gazed into an old fashioned, but otherwise ordinary living room decorated with carved wood furniture and upholstery of a bygone era. An elaborately carved mantelpiece spoke of days of opulence, probably soon after the first world war when art nouveaux was the design optimum of the day. A large painting looked as though it had fallen in front of the mantel, probably from the wall above.

Despite the apparent inactivity of the house, Father Joshua proceeded cautiously. He had seen too much in his day to assume that a single reading of the rite of exorcism would completely clear the house. The tricks of the devil could almost be predictable. He was not going to be lulled into a false sense of security so easily. He hovered on the threshold of the open front door.

"Father Michael!" he called in a loud whisper. He heard no sound to indicate that anyone was in the house. He called a second time.

"Father Michael! Can you hear me? It's Father Joshua!"

Father Joshua listened closely. He heard nothing. No voice, no movement. He kept his left hand on the doorframe to remind himself to remain outside of the room directly in front of him. He had hoped to have Father Michael to assist him before entering the house, but with no sign of the other priest, he had no other option than to work on his own. He wasn't ready to step into the enemy's stronghold just yet. First, he returned to his car and taking his cell phone from the passenger seat, he dialed the Bishop's number.

A crackling noise met his ear instead of the usual ring. He

pulled the phone away quickly, then tried another number. That one also resulted in a loud static. He let out an exasperated breath.

"I've seen that movie too," he muttered, turning and giving the house a steady glare. "You'll have to do better than that if you want to rattle me."

Father Michael breathed deeply to keep himself calm. The room was pitch black. A demon lurked somewhere in the darkness, mocking him with laughter. He still had his bottle of holy water, mostly full, held under his left arm. Going by feel, he opened the bottle and poured a little into his hand, sprinkling it around himself randomly. He held no delusions about the strength of the evil spirit who had lured him into its domain. For this spawn of Satan, Father Michael reverted to saying the litany in the original Latin.

"Crux sacra sit mihi lux! Nunquam draco sit mihi dux. Vade retro Satana! Nunquam suade mihi vana! Sunt mala quae libas. Ipse venena bibas!"

He repeated this phrase several times, running the translation through his mind, "May the holy cross be my light! May the dragon never be my guide. Be gone Satan! Never tempt me with your vanities! What you offer me is evil. Drink the poison yourself!"

He closed the bottle of holy water and reached into one of his deep pockets, wrapping his hand around a cross he always carried with him at exorcisms. It had been a gift from his mother while he was at seminary. A beautiful, ornately designed cross of pure silver, six inches high. It had probably cost a small fortune. Whatever superstitions might attach to the precious metal, it somehow felt right to now to take it out and hold it up in defiance of the demon.

A miniscule glint of red against the silver as he held the cross in front of him alerted Father Michael to a breech in the darkness. A pair of red, glowing eyes that blinked open, then closed again, returning the complete void. Father Michael pushed his arm out in the direction he had seen that evil glint, holding the cross aloft.

"Crux sacra sit mihi lux! Nunquam draco sit mihi dux. Vade retro Satana! Nunquam suade mihi vana! Sunt mala quae libas. Ipse venena bibas!" he repeated again.

His hand began to feel warm, then grew hotter. A red radiance slowly intensified from the cross in his hand, yet he was reluctant to drop it. A moment later, it was too late. The hot metal seared his flesh, welding skin and silver together so that the priest could not let go. He screamed in agony and shook his hand, trying to let it drop. The cross was stuck fast to his palm.

The glowing silver cross began to melt. Flames danced across the top of the crossbeam and the bottom of the longer bar began to elongate, forming a sharp point at the base. Father Michael remembered the holy water. He shifted the bottle to under his right arm and opened it with his free hand, then poured a generous amount over the blazing metal. It began to cool. The radiant glow faded. The pain receded a little, though the burning sensation would not so easily be quenched. Father Michael's nerves throbbed madly with pain, though he knew it was imperative that he keep his thinking facilities clear.

A knocking noise riveted his attention to the direction he was sure he had seen the glowing eyes. Had the demon taken on physical form? Such things were not unknown. Father Michael began the Latin litany once again under his breath, slowly approaching a shape he sensed in the darkness. A small amount of light had begun to penetrate the total gloom from the afterglow of the cross, as if a door had opened onto the shadows of the night. A form became scarcely discernable, a black mass against an otherworldly dark miasma.

Father Michael crept towards the enemy, murmuring the Latin phrases under his breath. He gripped the welded cross tightly in his palm, despite the burning pain, as he drew closer to the shape, nerves on edge. It didn't retreat, but appeared to move towards him. The priest was determined to vanquish the enemy, even if God required that he grapple with Satan himself in hand-to-hand combat. With a final shout of the last line of the litany, he plunged the dagger into the mass, meeting resistance as if he pierced flesh.

"IPSE VENENA BIBAS!"

A very human-sounding scream resounded through the room, then the beam of a flashlight pierced the darkness and Father Michael saw, not Satan, but another priest bleeding from the dagger wound he had inflicted.

"God forgive me!" he shouted, as the flashlight fell from Father Joshua's hand.

Chapter Eleven

Raymond released Tesha's arm and directed his flashlight to add his beam to her failing light.

"I don't suppose you brought extra batteries, did you?"

"That would have been smart," Tesha lamented. "I didn't think we would be here this long."

"None of us did." For once, Raymond didn't sound the least bit antagonistic to Tesha. He scanned his light around the impossibly intact passageway. It looked much the same as it had before the ceiling had collapsed.

Tesha gave it a wary glance, distrusting the unpredictable rooms.

"How can this be possible? Phillip..." Tears sprang to her eyes again. She hadn't finished wiping her cheeks of the previous ones.

"None of this is possible. It is what it is though. Phillip would want me to get you out of here alive."

Tesha looked towards the door they had just come through.

"You don't suppose..."

"No," Raymond snapped, setting his jaw. "I don't. My

brother is gone. I think we should try to retrace our steps. Maybe that way we'll find the way out."

Raymond began examining the wall with his fingers as well as his eyes, looking for the opening to the bookcase door they had entered through before. With inadequate light, Tesha attempted to help by knocking on the walls, listening for a change of tone. She had always had a good sense of direction and was reasonably sure which way the passage the door had been. After a few moments, a change in resonance told her she had found it.

"Over here!" she called to Raymond.

They pushed the door open together, straining against the weight of many books on the shelves on the other side. Raymond brought out his flashlight and shone it on the bookcase door. It was the same one. They had found it! They crept forward cautiously, prepared to discover any kind of changes inside the room.

The study looked just as it had before the tremor that had disturbed the books and furnishings earlier. Tesha took a tentative look around the room, making her way slowly to the door on the other side that she remembered led to a hallway and the ghostly ballroom. Her flashlight wasn't quite dead, but the dim beam made her cautious about bumping into things. She looked at the far door suspiciously. Would it still go where it had before? She didn't trust anything about this house anymore.

Meanwhile, Raymond had begun exploring the room, scanning his light here and there, looking for any other secret doors or clues to explain the strange phenomena they had experienced and perhaps what might have happened to Dylan. He appeared fascinated by some of the old-fashioned objects displayed; a ship in a bottle, an antique crystal brandy decanter and especially a large, sepia-toned world globe with outdated country borders painted over it.

"Hey Tesha, look at this!" Raymond held up what Tesha assumed was an Edwardian period walking stick of mahogany wood, topped with a filigree silver pommel. Raymond suddenly pulled it apart to reveal a sword inside.

Tesha gasped. She had heard of such things as sword canes, but she had never actually seen one. As far as she knew, they were illegal, though it was probably worth a fortune in an antique market.

Awestruck with the beauty of the piece, Tesha glided over to where Raymond stood with the sword cane, turning her back on the suspect door for a moment. Raymond clicked the sword back inside its casing and handed the walking stick to Tesha for her to examine.

"I wonder if..." Tesha began. "It could be worth having a weapon with us. Would taking something from the house bind us to it in some way?"

She wandered back towards the door, still holding the precious antique. She didn't see Raymond's shrug. Tesha carefully pulled the sword from its secret rod and examined the sharp edge in the flickering glint of Raymond's moving flashlight beam. The blade had some sort of etching on it, but she couldn't make it out in the semi-darkness.

She turned towards Raymond, opening her mouth to speak, but the words were lost as her eyes opened wide in horror. Behind Raymond, the wall itself was moving. A shape formed, like a giant face with its mouth opened in a silent scream. Two appendages stretched out from the fabric of the wallpaper, reaching for Raymond.

Tesha pointed to the wall and was about to scream in warning, but Raymond looked up at her and seeing the terror on her face, he dived into a roll across the floor towards her, turning just in time to see the tentacle-like protrusions recede back into the wallpaper and the face slowly flatten until the wall looked smooth again.

"What the f..." Before Raymond could finish his shocked exclamation, a cacophony of high-pitched screeches assaulted their ears and a hoard of small, two-legged creatures poured out from under the desk, running straight towards Tesha and Raymond. Raymond froze in confusion for a moment, watching what looked like some sort of Eastern evil spirit creatures dressed in red and gold kilts and breastplates, their faces made up in black, red and gold to show angry, long-fanged demonic frowns meant to frighten the superstitious.

"*Rakshama!*" Tesha shouted as she swung the sword in her hand to defend herself from the swarming sprites. She hit the first one with the flat of the blade, knocking it several feet away from her, but it only returned to attack again. The sharp edge came down on the second one and the creature exploded into tiny fragments that dissipated into the air.

Raymond kicked several of them away while Tesha sliced through more as they came within range. She quickly worked out that she could do a sideways slice and eliminate several at once, each of them exploding into tiny, dissipating particles. Unfortunately she had to crouch to get that angle, which made dancing away from their attempts to flank her difficult.

It soon became apparent that the demon-creatures were specifically targeting Tesha. Raymond defended her back, side-kicking some of the creatures all the way across the room. Within just a few minutes, the hoard thinned and Tesha could see she and Raymond were winning, but then three rushed her from different directions at the same time. Tesha dispatched one and Raymond punted another. The third made it past the lethal blade long enough to bite Tesha on the calf of her left leg.

She screamed in pain and sliced through the offending creature, nearly cutting herself in the process. Then she went on the offensive with her sword and finished off the few stragglers, ignoring the throbbing pain in her leg.

Tesha and Raymond stopped and looked around the room with Raymond's flashlight, searching for any hidden entities. Tesha tried to shine her fading light in other directions, but it soon went dead. They stood for a few moments, breathing heavily, alert for anything that might come at them next. After a few moments, they began to get their breath and Tesha broke the silence.

"Do you watch a lot of Jackie Chan movies or something? Those were pretty impressive kicks!"

Raymond chuckled.

"I take Karate lessons on Saturdays. I'm going for my brown belt next month."

Tesha nodded, taking in the information.

"I never knew."

"Yeah, well," Raymond responded. "We haven't really made an effort to get to know each other. You were Phillip's friend."

At the mention of Phillip, Tesha scrunched her face as if she would cry again.

"What *were* those things?" Raymond asked, hoping to distract her. "I've never seen anything like them, even in D&D manuals."

"Rakshasas," Tesha explained. "They come from Hindu mythology, though they're usually bigger."

"Usually? Is this what you do with *your* Saturdays?"

Tesha laughed in a jerking fashion through the tears that

spilled over her lashes, holding back the hysteria.

"My grandparents and aunts have told me traditional stories since I was very little. Rakshasas were created from the breath of Brahma when he was asleep at the end of the Satya Yuga, but as soon as they were created, they were so filled with bloodlust that they started eating Brahma himself. Brahma shouted *Rakshama!* which is Sanskrit for *Protect me!* and Vishnu came to his aid, banishing to Earth all Rakshasas. In another story, Ravana kidnapped Rama's wife, Sita, and took her off to his stronghold, Lanka. Rama, aided by the monkey King Sugriva and his army of monkeys, laid siege to Lanka, then slew Ravana, and rescued Sita."

"Great, so can we expect an army of monkeys to come out next?"

"I think not. We vanquished the Rakshasas ourselves."

Raymond looked thoughtful for a moment.

"It's interesting that they targeted you, just like the tentacle thing from the wall targeted me. I read Lovecraft."

"Sooo... we're seeing malevolent things from our familiar mythologies?"

"It would seem so," Raymond agreed. "Maybe if my family was more religious, I'd be getting attacked by more Biblical-type demons."

"Be careful what you wish for." Tesha's eyes opened wide in alarm. She looked left and right, seeking any movement in the shadows of the room that might present a threat.

"That's what Ava always says." Raymond frowned and looked down. "I wonder if she's alright."

"And Dylan too," Tesha added. "I wonder if any of us are

94

going to be alright."

An awkward silence settled between them, then Tesha brought up the one fear in her mind that at least had a human shape to it.

"Raymond, you like Ava, don't you?"

A smile flickered on his lips.

"Phillip's been talking."

"Don't you think she's a little young? I mean, she's just turned fourteen."

"And I'm almost eighteen, I know. Makes me look like a perve. That's why I've never asked her out. I don't think her parents let her date yet anyway."

Raymond turned and looked Tesha in the eye.

"But you don't have to worry. Ava's a smart girl. I admire that. When she's eighteen, I'll be twenty-one. Okay nearly twenty-two. But what I'm saying is that I can wait for her to grow up. I'm not a baby-raper."

Tesha nodded, accepting his explanation. The irony was not lost on her, that she was only here because she had come to protect Ava from any unwanted advances from Raymond. Apparently it hadn't been necessary, but she chose not to tell Raymond she had been concerned.

Raymond changed the subject.

"We have to get out of here before we worry about any of that. We don't know what's on the other side of that door or if it will be the same as it was before, but there's nowhere else for us to go. Are you ready to give it a try?"

Tesha nodded again.

"Just keep that sword handy," Raymond advised. "You're pretty good with it."

That brought a smile to Tesha's face. She had to admit to herself that the weapon felt good in her hand. She picked up the cane-sheath and stuck it in her belt, but kept the blade ready as they sauntered over to the door that had led to the hallway to the ghostly ballroom before.

Raymond gave her a questioning glance, as if to ask if she was ready. Tesha nodded, gripping the handle of the sword and turning her gaze towards the door. Raymond turned the knob and opened it slowly.

Ava reached her aunt's house just as the town clock was striking eleven o'clock. She hoped Aunt Laurie hadn't gone to bed yet. Ava knew her aunt had an interest in the occult, but she had never spoken of what she did for Halloween, or Samhain as she called it, in Ava's presence. Ava assumed her parents had insisted on keeping much of Aunt Laurie's interests away from hers and Dylan's ears.

She was not surprised to see the porch light was out. Trick-or-treating generally finished by nine o'clock, even for the bigger kids. Ava tried to look through her aunt's windows to see if there was a light on in any of the rooms. With the curtains shut, she couldn't see much, but she thought she caught a flicker, perhaps of candlelight or a television screen, past the edge of the curtain. It appeared to be somewhere beyond the front living room.

Still unsure, Ava tried knocking very lightly so that she wouldn't wake Aunt Laurie if she had gone to bed or fallen asleep watching a late night movie. She waited a few minutes, then began to wonder if her knock had been *too* light, impossible to hear from beyond the front room. She raised her hand up and was about to knock just a little louder, when the curtain flickered.

Ava craned her neck, trying to see if her aunt was looking out the corner of the window, but then the door opened.

"A little late for trick-or-treating, isn't it Ava?" Aunt Laurie looked as if a scolding was building up behind her clear, green eyes. Ava suddenly remembered that she was in costume.

"I... I'm supposed to be at a party," she stammered. "But something's gone wrong. Can I come in?"

Laurie's expression changed to one of concern and she stepped back to allow her niece inside. Ava glanced around the familiar living room, all the walls covered with shelves and cupboards and even a tallboy chest that would normally be appropriate in a bedroom. The plush oriental carpet was the same dark green as the walls and drying herbs hung from baskets attached to the ceiling in one corner of the room. Laurie's furniture was more for comfort or storage than for show and the two natural linen double sofas facing each other in the middle of the room created a comforting, amiable atmosphere.

"Shall I make some tea and we can sit down and talk about it?" That was Aunt Laurie, always ready to listen.

"Actually, it's kind of urgent," Ava blurted out.

Aunt Laurie looked at her niece in a funny sort of way, as if assessing something Ava couldn't see.

"You've got time for a small cup. Now sit down and tell me

all about it."

Ava obeyed, sitting at her aunt's small table in the kitchen while Aunt Laurie poured a cup of tea from a pot she had just brewed. Before it even had a chance to cool, the words came tumbling out and Ava told Aunt Laurie everything.

Chapter Twelve

Patrick Williamson was no coward, but he was also no hero. What he was, however, was a decent human being who couldn't let an unwary noob security guard fall victim to the evil of Number 23 Hazelwood Avenue alone on the night of Halloween.

He took a swig from his can of light beer. He had promised himself he would only have the one. He didn't want to have alcohol in his blood if he decided to go ahead with the intention that had tormented him since the day before, when the mayor had told him that a security guard was to be sent out alone to *that* house. Williamson didn't consider himself to be particularly brave, but his conscience would not abate. He had seen for himself what awaited the unwary guard. No man should have to face that kind of evil alone and unprepared.

The question was, did he have the guts to go near that house again? Williamson looked at his hand holding the aluminum can, shaking hard enough that he could hear the liquid inside slosh violently. He put the can down and laced his fingers together with those of his other hand, willing the involuntary tremor to stop. He began wringing his hands together instead, asking himself if he would actually be capable of doing any good.

He had kept the drinking under control for two years now. Williamson's job at City Hall hadn't been affected by the months after that night he quit doing security, except that he couldn't stop himself telling the story of what happened that night every Halloween. The mayor was the only one who took him seriously. The others at work enjoyed listening to his rants, treating it like a ghost story meant for entertainment. People just didn't want to believe that demons could be real, even deeply religious folk.

He took a cigarette out of the pack sitting on the cheap table in front of him and tried to hold it steady, long enough to flick his cigarette lighter and hold the flame at the end of the ciggie. It took a few seconds, but he managed to get it lit. He always managed. Whatever he had to. The run down apartment he lived in might not be much, but it was a roof over his head and he got to work on time every day. Sometimes it was enough.

Williamson shut off his internal dialogue, upended the beer can and got up, grabbing his car keys off the table. No more excuses. He was going out to that house, if for no other reason than to warn the guy on duty that he absolutely must not set foot inside, no matter what he saw or heard.

A short drive later, he was on Hazelwood Avenue. Williamson had intended to park in front of the house, but there were too many cars parked in front of it already. He presumed one would be the security guard's car, but he furrowed his brow as he passed the other two black sedans and pulled up in front of the house next door.

When he got out of the car and looked towards the house, he thought he saw something moving in front of Number 23. He stood by his car for a moment, letting his eyes adjust to the low street lighting. There were two shapes moving in front of the porch of the house. Williamson assumed that one would be the security guard, probably stopping some kid from trying to get inside.

He started to trot towards the dark shapes, but when he got as far as the overgrown lawn and could see them closer up, he stopped in his tracks. He felt the blood leave his face and a strange tingle flushed through his body. He tried to step backwards, but his feet wouldn't obey.

The taller of the figures turned towards him. All Williamson could see of it was a long, black robe with a pointed hood and the glint of streetlights reflected from the blade of a long scythe. The smaller figure, a white skeleton, began to dance towards him.

A scream began building from the bottom of his chest. His mouth opened. Then suddenly a distinctively southern accent drawled from the taller figure.

"Stop it, Lashawn, I'm scared enough without you dancin' round like some spook outta that house yourself!"

The voice sounded young. The figure turned towards Williamson.

"Sorry Mister, my brother's coo-yahn sometimes. You the security guard?"

Williamson took a few deep breaths, slowly working out that these were just a couple of kids in Halloween costumes. He was able to walk now and as he drew closer, he saw that they were African-American. Their dark skin had made the costumes far too effective under the circumstances.

"No," he answered a heartbeat later. "I came to look for him."

"We did too. My friend, Raymond, was coming here with some other kids and I tried to talk him outta it, but he ain't come back to the party so I was gettin' worried."

He turned to look at the house.

"This ain't no place to be foolin' round. I don't care who

thinks I'm capo, I ain't goin' inside!"

"Capo?" Williamson scrunched his brows, not comprehending some of the strange terms.

"Coward," the tall boy supplied. My family moved here from New Orleans when I was fifteen. Raymond was my first friend."

"Coo-yahn means actin' like a fool!" Lashawn supplied, beaming a big grin and dancing again in his black satin costume with skeleton bones painted on it. Someone had done a good job of painting a white skull mask onto his face as well. "Joseph always tellin' me I'm crazy as a Chaoui. That's a raccoon! They get into ev'rything!"

"You're Joseph?" Williamson asked the tall boy.

"Yep. Joseph Despre. This is my brother, Lashawn. He's only thirteen and should be goin' home now, since we can't find Jerry."

Joseph gave his brother a pointed look.

"Oh, man!" Lashawn whined. "I wanted to see inside the house!"

"No way, Lashawn, you get yourself home. Nobody's goin' inside that house. Tell Mama I'll be along soon."

Lashawn hung his head, dejected.

"You be home in an hour or Mama will have the cops out after you!" Lashawn threatened.

"You make sure she does," Joseph said. "If I'm not back by then, I got trouble." He pushed his brother's back to send him on his way. Lashawn danced down the street, performing his skeleton impersonation for any houses with a light still on in case someone might look out a window.

"I wouldn't come with Raymond," Joseph explained. "I tried to tell Jerry not to watch this place alone, but he needed the money."

Williamson took a cigarette out of a pack in his shirt pocket and lit it, calmer now in the company of Joseph.

"We were both too sensible to come here, yet here we are!" he chuckled, watching as Joseph's little brother disappeared around a corner. "My name's Patrick Williamson. Pleased to meet someone else as crazy or, how did your brother say it? Coo-yahn, as me."

Joseph grinned at Williamson's quick grasp of the Cajun slang, then his smile dropped and his eyes looked troubled.

"We're goin' in, ain't we?" he asked, still looking down the street where Lashawn had gone.

Williamson took a deep drag from his cigarette and blew it out slowly.

"I don't see how we've got any choice."

Father Michael pressed his left hand against the wound as hard as he could to try to stop the bleeding. Pulling the dagger out with his fused right hand had caused him pain beyond imagining, but he had managed it through the adrenaline shock of discovering what he had done.

"I'm so, so sorry! You are Father Joshua, aren't you?"

"And you must be Father Michael," the older priest responded with an assiduous calm. "It's not the most propitious introduction I've had to another priest."

"The demon showed himself, then you were there instead." Father Michael had tears in his eyes as he tried to explain.

"The enemy has many tricks," Father Joshua acknowledged. "Thank God you missed the heart."

"But you're bleeding so much!"

"If I should die in the service of the Lord, it is God's will. Help me sit up." Father Joshua started to struggle, causing the bleeding to flow freely again. Father Michael helped to prop him up, then resumed pressing on the wound. He had nothing with him to use as a bandage beyond the fabric of the priest's cassock.

"We never should have tried to do this on Halloween." Father Michael shook his head slowly.

"The fault is mine," Father Joshua admitted. "I underestimated the nature of the entity we're dealing with. This is no discarnate soul playing such tricks on us."

"We should call the Bishop."

"No use trying to phone anyone. Cell phones won't work. We're on our own." Father Joshua looked up at Father Michael, the spark of life weakening in his eyes.

"I still have holy water," Father Michael said with forced enthusiasm. "We can get out of here and come back at a more auspicious time."

Father Joshua nodded weakly.

"We can try. I brought holy water as well. Let's hope it's enough."

Father Joshua struggled to stand up. Father Michael gave him his arm to lean on, while still pressing the wound with his other hand. The bleeding worried him, but there was no other choice. He couldn't leave the other priest alone in the house. Emergency services might never even be able to get in. There was no way to call for help. Father Joshua had been right, they were completely on their own.

But still with God, Father Michael thought silently.

"When I first came to the house," Father Michael reminded them both. "Holy water served to get the doors and windows to open. Perhaps it will work again to get us out."

Father Joshua nodded.

"I will apply it along the way and hold the flashlight, since your hands are otherwise occupied. It is to our advantage that the entity, or entities, didn't want us inside in the first place. Perhaps they will be happy to expel us."

Father Joshua mumbled blessings in Latin as he sprinkled holy water on the path before them and on the door. Neither of the priests had wandered very far through the house, but Father Michael was surprised when they made their way through the doorway Father Joshua had come through and found themselves in the living room. He was sure there had been another room in between.

Soft light found its way through the windows at the front of the house. Father Joshua was about to pour more holy water into his hand when the front door blasted open, a chorus of tortured voices augmenting the dramatic force bursting outwards. The elder priest continued to bleed, despite Father Michael's attempts to staunch his wound. As they passed through the open door, he stumbled. Father Michael was sure he heard a deep, rumbling laughter echoing from the walls.

It was instinct more than anything else that made him suddenly shove the elderly priest forward through the doorway, just as the door slammed. He nearly lost his footing at the edge of the porch, sending them both stumbling to the ground, but Father Joshua grabbed a post by the steps, dropping his flashlight, and helped the younger priest regain balance for both of them. Father Michael left the flashlight where it fell. They had no further need for it now.

They were out of the house, but not yet completely safe. Father Michael looked askance at the long grass covering the front lawn, waving in the flashlight beam as if there were a breeze when he felt none. The cars were parked just where they had left them, yet another car had parked closely in front of the senior priest's Ford. Father Michael couldn't tell the model or exact color in the dim lighting, but it looked like a light colored Chevy of an older model.

Technically it was parked in front of the house next door, but the close proximity bothered Father Michael. Surely no one else had come to this forsaken property on such a night? There was no time to contemplate possibilities. Father Joshua had already lost far too much blood.

"Father, I think you should continue sprinkling the holy water all the way to the car. There's something moving in the grass and it's not the wind. Father Joshua nodded and poured more holy water into his hand, sprinkling it in front of him as they staggered down the stairs as best they could. Father Michael couldn't help thinking that Father Joshua was looking older and weaker every moment. He opened his mouth to respond, but the effort cost him too dearly and he only nodded again.

Father Michael heard the distinctive hissing of snakes as they made their way across the lawn towards his car, but the holy water appeared to be effective, holding the slithering spawns of Satan back as the priests passed. They got within a few steps of Father Michael's car when Father Joshua collapsed. Father Michael caught him, but the bottle of holy water fell to the ground, spilling its contents.

The sudden flood worked in their favor. The undulating grass leaned away from them as if they were a whirlwind and father Michael dragged the unconscious priest the remaining few steps to the car door. He leaned him up against the car to get the door open and though it took a struggle, got him into the seat and belted in. Father Michael rushed to the driver's side and began to pray that he would be able to get the older priest to a hospital before he bled to death, with only one hand free to try to slow the bleeding as best he could and that one obstructed by a painful burning and a fused silver cross.

Chapter Thirteen

Tesha and Raymond peered out into the dark hallway. All was silent. The calliope music had stopped, though Tesha was braced for it to start up again. The hallway looked much as it had before with the paintings along the walls, the small table with the burning oil lamp, a door at each end and an open archway between that led to the room where they had seen the ghostly dancers. Both Tesha and Raymond wondered privately if they would see the same room there now.

They crept slowly, as if there were something that might hear their footsteps and be alerted to their presence. They reached the open archway and peered around the wall with trepidation. Tesha's mouth dropped open and her eyes opened wide. She couldn't see Raymond's expression, but she expected he would be similarly amazed at the transformation.

The room looked the same size and shape as before. The chandelier still hung in the same place, lit by candles as it had been previously. However, the walls were now a deep, blood red shade and the shining hardwood floors were mostly covered with a large area rug in a black and purple harlequin design. Neither of them had ever seen anything like it. It was as if someone had come and redecorated the room in the time since they had last passed through.

"This is impossible," Raymond muttered.

"A lot about this house is impossible." Tesha gripped the edge of the wall, unable to convince herself to step into the room. Raymond showed no sign of continuing into the room yet either.

"That door should lead to the dining room." Raymond pointed to the familiar door across the room.

"Then what," Tesha squawked. Her irritation with the inexplicable phenomena was beginning to show. "We tried to get back to the living room before and it brought us here!"

"We must have got turned around somehow." Raymond's eyes darted around the suspect room. Tesha didn't believe his assertion for a moment and didn't think he did either. Trying to make sense of the nonsensical hadn't served them well so far. She searched her imaginative mind for any ideas for another approach, but could think of nothing more practical than Raymond's suggestion.

"Okay, let's try it." Tesha forced her hands to let go of the wall. "But if that carnival music starts up again, you better keep up because I'm a fast runner!"

An amused smirk flickered at the corner of Raymond's mouth, but his only response was a nod of agreement. Under the circumstances, running struck him as a perfectly logical move.

Tesha led, moving at a fast creep. Her soft-soled shoes were silent against the carpet. Her mind said the shortest distance between two points is a straight line, but her more primal instincts directed her feet to stay close to the wall, away from the center of the room. Raymond shadowed her, keeping alert for anything that might happen.

The blessed silence was vanquished when they got about half way. Rather than the calliope music they had heard before, a sustained, dark chord from what sounded like a pipe organ filled the room. Tesha recognized it as a D-minor, the same chord that opened the theme to Andrew Lloyd Webber's musical version of *The Phantom of the Opera*. However, when the tune eventually progressed, it followed the beginning of Johann Sebastian Bach's *Tocatta and Fugue in D-minor*, yet played in a more discordant key.

A squeal of terror escaped Tesha's lips and she sprinted to run, but all of a sudden the floor began to move from side to side, segments approximately a foot wide alternating in opposite directions like a carnival funhouse floor trick. Raymond tried to stay close to her and reached for her hand at one point, but the movement of the floor under their feet prevented contact.

The motion became more chaotic with every step, moving up and down as well as sideways. The music sounded louder as they advanced, reaching ear-splitting volume before they were halfway. They negotiated each step, one at a time, progressing gradually across the undulating floorboards.

Raymond made it to the door first. He shoved it open and chose his moment to leap across the threshold onto solid ground, then turned and shouted back to Tesha.

"Focus on the next plank, take one at a time and try not to panic!"

Tesha remembered Raymond's Karate lessons. She summoned courage from every martial arts film she had ever seen and tried to breathe deeply and keep focus on the next step, then the next. The room felt endless. She could almost swear it was elongating as she moved forwards.

At last she got within two planks of the door, but the floorboard raised like an ocean wave and she lost her balance, rolling backwards. Tesha sprang up to her feet as quickly as she was able to on the unsteady ground. When she made her way near to the door again, Raymond's arm shot out.

"Grab my hand! Jump!" he called to her, though she could hardly hear him over the deafening music.

Tesha saw the segment in front of her reversing to the right and jumped, turning her body also to the right. She used the motion to help propel her second step to leap towards Raymond. The floor raised up again, but this time their hands connected and Raymond pulled Tesha through the doorway, her body sliding over the hardwood flooring wave just before it slapped against the top of the doorframe with an almighty thwack!

Her full weight propelled towards Raymond might have knocked him over, but he spun, again using what he had learned in his lessons in Karate, not only clearing her of the doorway faster but distributing the oncoming weight in a circular motion that allowed them both to regain their balance within a couple of seconds.

"Don't freak," Raymond warned her before Tesha had turned her gaze from the gouge the sudden whip of floor had left in the top of the doorframe. Her stomach felt sick, just thinking of what it might have done to her if Raymond hadn't pulled her through so quickly.

She turned and let out a sudden gasp. The dining room itself was unchanged. There was the same massive oak dining table, the same carved wood chairs, even the same space on the wall where something had been moved. With just Raymond's flashlight stuck in his belt since the ordeal of the previous room, it was thankfully too dim to read the writing presumed to be in blood on the back wall, though Tesha knew it was still there.

The difference that had brought a gasp from Tesha was that the dining table was now occupied. Expensive looking china plates and gleaming silverware were set in four of the eight available place settings. On the beautiful, fine embroidered tapestry chair cushions sat two adult and two child-sized skeletons. They were posed with their empty eye sockets directed at their plates, as if a family had sat down to dinner and were completely unaware of their frightened visitors.

Tesha turned to Raymond about to say something, then she looked past him and the thought slipped from her mind.

"Did you close the door?"

Raymond turned, seeing that the door behind them had shut.

"No," he answered. "At least I don't think I did. Maybe I did it without noticing in all the excitement."

Tesha looked up, meeting Raymond's eyes.

"Do you suppose if we open it, there might be another room again? Maybe even the living room like it was before?" The quaver in her voice belied the hopeful sound in her words.

Raymond's eyes darted around the room a moment before he answered, taking in the doorway to the left that appeared to go into a kitchen and the closed door on the right. He flicked a quick glance at the skeletons before looking away again quickly.

"I suppose there's one way to find out. Ready?"

Tesha nodded and stepped back, giving Raymond plenty of room to react to whatever might happen and herself space to run if necessary. He turned the knob and opened the door halfway. Through the opening, Tesha saw the harlequin pattern still on the floor raising from the far end of the room and rushing towards them as if in a giant wave about to ram into them. Raymond slammed the door, grabbed Tesha by the shoulders and moved them both across the room to the far wall.

They stood for a moment while Raymond took several sharp breaths and Tesha tried not to think of the dark writing on the wall behind them. Every muscle in Raymond's body was tensed, ready to run if the floor wave crashed through the wall. A few seconds passed in silence, then when nothing happened, they began to relax. Tesha let out an audible sigh.

At that moment, the skull of one of the adult skeletons turned towards them, as if it were regarding them with the hollow recesses where its eyes should be. The end of the sigh transformed into a whimper as the other three skulls twisted towards them and Tesha bounded through the open doorway into a kitchen with hanging pans on the wall. Raymond followed close behind, shining his flashlight in front of himself.

Tesha stopped suddenly, causing Raymond to bash into her. He shone his light forward to see a knife block quivering. The large kitchen knives slid out of the block as if an invisible hand controlled them. Tesha didn't wait to discover their intentions, but turned and shoved Raymond, racing to get out of the kitchen. She yelped at the sight of the skeletons, still facing them and following their progress, and ran for the closed door at the other end of the room.

Raymond tried to catch up to open it first and look for danger, but Tesha was running scared and for a small girl, she could move fast in a panic. She pulled the door open, dropping her weight to heave it open quickly and started to run through, then she bounced back a step and let out an ear-splitting belly scream.

Chapter Fourteen

"You can go in and see him now. This way." The nurse led Father Michael to a semi-private room with two hospital beds inside. One of them was unoccupied. Father Joshua was talking into his cell phone with his good hand. The other one was restricted by the bandaging over his shoulder, protecting the stab wound. Father Michael looked down at the bandaging on his own right hand, where the silver cross had been fused to his flesh. It had taken surgery to remove it, but as it wasn't life threatening, the doctors had treated him on an outpatient basis, giving him some salve to prevent infection from the burn.

He waited patiently while Father Joshua finished his phone call.

"Yes, Your Excellency, I understand. Is there no one else? Father Michael has endured a harrowing night already."

Father Joshua paused, listening to a response, then he asked one last question.

"Would you like to speak to him yourself? He's just come in." Another short pause. "Yes, yes I see. I'll tell him. Goodbye, Your Excellency."

Father Joshua looked up at Father Michael. His eyes still

looked weak, but he seemed otherwise no worse than tired. Luckily he had a common blood type and the hospital had been adequately supplied to replace what he had lost.

"The Bishop is coming to meet you here," he explained. "He's hoping you'll feel up to returning to the house with him, but he doesn't want anyone else meeting at the property. It's too dangerous."

"He's coming here personally?" Father Michael tried to subdue his obvious surprise.

"His Excellency has some experience with exorcisms himself. He wasn't always a Bishop! He understands the gravity of the situation now and doesn't want to leave the house unprotected, since we don't know what's happened to the security guard."

Father Michael nodded, taking in Father Joshua's justification. The thought of returning to Number 23 Hazelwood Avenue filled him with dread, but Father Michael recognized that it was his duty. This is what he had been trained for. This was how God had called him to His service.

Father Joshua filled the momentary silence with a show of concern.

"How is your hand?" He looked at the bandaged hand with something that looked like sympathy.

"They put something on it to numb the pain, for now," Father Michael answered. "It is nothing compared to your own injury."

"Pah! At least the dagger was cold." Father Joshua looked away, conscious that Father Michael might still feel guilt for wielding the offending weapon.

"His Excellency will discuss with you how to proceed."

Father Michael could see that the other priest was tiring.

"I'll leave you to rest, then. I'll tell the staff that His Excellency can find me in the cafeteria. Is there anything I can bring you?"

The elder priest seemed to sink into his bed.

"Just a good report of success," he uttered in a low, croaking voice. His eyes closed and Father Michael assumed the senior priest had drifted into sleep. He stepped softly out of the room and asked directions to the cafeteria, leaving word that the Bishop would be coming to look for him. The thought crossed his mind that he had also promised to give a report to the mayor, but the phone number he had for him was for his office phone and no one would be there in the middle of the night. He would have to leave that until whatever happened when he returned to Number 23 with the Bishop had already occurred, presuming he lived through the night.

Joseph Despre and Patrick Williamson shared a mutual understanding. Neither of them wanted to be there. Both were terrified and sure that some kind of evil force existed in the house. Joseph had told Williamson about the lights he had seen in the upstairs windows, then Williamson had filled Joseph in on his experience of the house; the disorientation, the difficulty in finding their way out, the voices he had heard and Collins' part in securing their escape through prayer. He showed Joseph the gold cross he wore beneath the collar of his T-shirt.

They agreed to stay close together and if possible, to conduct their respective rescues without losing sight of the front door. They both acknowledged that the probability of sticking with that resolve was pretty low. They hoped the people they sought to find would answer verbal calls. Joseph had already tried reaching Raymond with his cell phone. It had gone straight to recorded message.

Reluctantly, they approached the front door. Williamson took the lead with Joseph staying close enough behind like a shadow. Williamson started to turn the doorknob, his old security guard flashlight at the ready.

"I wish you had thought to bring a flashlight too. We don't know what we're going to find in there and the more light, the better."

Joseph silently agreed with Williamson, but he had come straight from the Halloween party and hadn't had a chance to prepare. At least his costume had been no more than a rubber werewolf mask, which he had intentionally left behind.

"I'll warn you now," he said. If a spider come outta there, you gonna hear me scream like a little girl. We got some nasty spiders in New Orleans. Brown recluse, two different kinds of black widow and brown widows, all deadly poisonous. We got ordinary house spiders too but you won't see me get near 'em!"

Williamson's chuckle reduced the tension a little.

"If we don't see anything worse that a few spiders, I'll be happy. Black widows are everywhere in this country but I'm not planning on sticking my hand into any dark places."

He pushed the door open slowly, alert for anything out of place. The old style carved wood furniture and old flowered wallpaper looked just as it had the first time he had made the mistake of setting foot in this house, except that the painting that had once hung over the mantelpiece was now on the floor. One corner of the heavy frame was broken. Williamson shook his head, imagining the hazard if anyone had been beneath it when it fell.

Joseph had pretty good vision in the dark, honed by a misspent youth hunting crayfish in the creek at night back home. The faded upholstery on the furniture was no more nor less than he had expected, but it was all new to him. He tipped the painting from its resting place far enough to look at the innocent-looking nature scene, then put it back while he tried to remember something his granny had told him about rabbits.

"Keep that front door open," Williamson commanded. As the adult of the pair and the only one who had been inside the house before, it seemed natural for him to take charge. Joseph sauntered over to the door and leaned on it, all too happy to have a clear path to a quick escape.

Williamson shone his light all around the room, then let out a big sigh when it landed on the door leading to the next room. He remembered a dining room behind the door. The moment he and the other security guard had entered it before, all had become confusion and they had struggled to find their way back out. His hand began to shake as memories flooded back. Some of them had been suppressed after the ordeal. Now he could see in his mind's eye the kitchen implements flying at them, himself and Collins moving a large display cabinet to block the open doorway where the knives and heavy objects were coming from. The terror of feeling trapped, unable to escape whatever malevolent force it was that tormented them, until Collins had saved them with his religious mumbo-jumbo.

Williamson still didn't think of himself as a churchy man, but his hand went to his neckline where the new, fourteen carat gold cross hung from a gold-colored chain. It was a concession to Collins' success. If it was all superstition, at least it was superstition that worked.

In many ways, the Bishop seemed like any other elderly man, albeit one with a regal bearing. He had come dressed appropriately in the red-striped black cassock befitting his rank in the church. Father Michael wondered about the man beneath the office. What had his name been before he joined the priesthood? Had he ever had a secular job? Many came to the church as young men, but others were called later in life. Father Michael himself had been thirty-two when he took the cloth.

The Bishop had introduced himself to Father Michael as Bishop Gregory, but most of the time Father Michael addressed him as *Your Excellency*, as custom demanded. When Father Michael asked if he had been an exorcist before he became a Bishop, the answer he had received surprised him. The Bishop had given him a simple 'no', explaining only that his services had been called elsewhere. Now Father Michael wondered what Father Joshua had meant when he had said that the Bishop had some experience with exorcisms, but it wasn't Father Michael's place to ask for further clarification.

Father Michael couldn't help noticing that the hands of the town clock tower were approaching midnight by the time he and the Bishop had discussed how to proceed back at the hospital, ascertained that Father Joshua was out of danger and driven back out to Hazelwood Avenue. It had been a long night already and now they were to begin again. Nothing Father Michael had said had swayed the Bishop to wait for morning.

To top things off, they had no sooner got out of their cars than a woman came storming from the house across the street with the protective hedge, charging straight towards them as if she had a complaint to lodge. She was wearing a heavy winter coat over what Father Michael assumed was her night clothes. All he could see was her stubby ankles and feet shoved into fluffy-toed slippers beneath the long coat. She had a scarf wrapped over her hair, which appeared to be wrapped up in old-fashioned papers for the night.

"Just what is going on in that house tonight?" she demanded in a brassy voice that scraped the ear like fingernails across a metal sheet. "I've seen far too many people going in there on this devil's night!"

How she could have managed to be curtain-twitching from behind that self-imposed barrier was a mystery to Father Michael in itself. He kept his voice calm and even as he answered her enquiry.

"You needn't concern yourself, Mrs..."

"Elwin," she supplied. "Natalie Elwin. I live over there." She turned and pointed at her house unnecessarily.

Father Michael nodded. The Bishop busied himself with placing various objects in his pockets, avoiding acknowledging the troublesome woman.

"The town mayor charged us with dealing with the house this Halloween, Mrs. Elwin. It's best if you go back home and leave it to us."

"To Catholics?" Mrs. Elwin all but sneered. "If Mayor Renick wants demons cast out of that evil house, he should have come to me! I can get the boys out here and we'll send those demons packing off to Hell where they belong with the power of Jesus!"

Father Michael and the Bishop exchanged a wary glance.

"You needn't trouble yourself," the Bishop cajoled the woman. He stepped towards her, raising a gentle hand to guide her back towards her house. "The church has professionally trained people for this and we have the matter in hand. Let me walk you to your house safely."

120

The Bishop's voice was so gentle that Father Michael was surprised when Mrs. Elwin set her jaw and looked as though she was about to object. She turned and began to walk back by herself with her elbows flying in exaggerated movement, then shouted back over her shoulder.

"I can walk ten steps by myself without help, thank you very much! But I'll get you boys some help. I know people!"

She disappeared around the hedge and the priests stood mutely, contemplating what the woman meant. After a moment, Father Michael broke the silence.

"What do you think she meant?"

The Bishop's shoulders sagged as he answered.

"I'm afraid we're going to be invaded by what is commonly referred to as 'the holy rollers'. I don't know what sect the woman belongs to, but I suggest we get on with this business before she can gather her forces and turn this into a three-ring circus. Perhaps we should go into the back yard to conduct our rituals."

Father Michael nodded his agreement and led the Bishop down the side path to the back yard, unconsciously leaning towards the wood fence away from the windows at the side of the house. He saw the necessity of avoiding interference from untrained people with more overconfidence than sense, but the house would block the street lights and leave them in shadow. He did not relish the thought of working in the dark.

Chapter Fifteen

Raymond glanced over his shoulder to make sure the skeletons sitting at the dining table weren't moving. Only the skulls had swivelled so far, watching his and Tesha's feeble attempts at escape. He directed his flashlight at the body that had caused Tesha to scream for only the briefest glance, enough to sear that image into his memory forever.

Most people knew each other in small towns. Raymond hadn't known Jerry Applegate well, but the vision of his body stuffed onto a cobweb-strewn storeroom shelf as if he had been there for months turned Raymond's stomach. The blood dripping from the shirt of Jerry's security guard uniform looked all too fresh. Worse, the musty utility room behind the door gave them nowhere to go. Raymond shut the door.

After gasping from the initial shock of seeing the security guard like that, Tesha began to hyperventilate. They had run out of options.

"We'll have to run through the kitchen," she choked out. "See what's on the other side!"

"We can't just run blind," Raymond reasoned. "Those knives might be what happened to the guard."

Tesha snapped her eyes up at Raymond. She hadn't thought of that possibility.

"Then what do we do?"

"We stay calm." Raymond hoped Tesha couldn't see how much his hand holding the flashlight was shaking. "Maybe..."

His eyes seemed to unfocus for a moment, then he looked towards the dining table.

"We could use a couple of chairs like shields."

Tesha turned and looked at the semi-animated skeletons, seemingly watching them with an eerie intensity.

"We won't get second chances."

"I know," Raymond acknowledged. "But we can't stay here. It's either try the door again, or go through the kitchen, like you said."

"Isn't there some way to just smash through the walls?" Tesha looked at Raymond with hope in her eyes. He gave it a moment's thought, then shook his head.

"We don't have tools. The table is made of wood and the legs wouldn't be strong enough. There has to be a door to the outside or a window somewhere."

Raymond's face screwed up into a confused expression.

"It just occurred to me... this is a two-storey house. Do you remember seeing stairs anywhere?"

Tesha searched her memory.

"No. No I don't. There should be some somewhere!"

Raymond nodded.

"Well they haven't been in any of the rooms we've seen. All the rooms upstairs should have windows. I think if we can get through the kitchen, we have to come to them. Grab a chair."

Raymond skirted around the all too interested skeletons and took one of the unoccupied chairs. The minute he picked it up, the adult skeleton that had first turned its head dropped its jaw bone and a thunderous moan echoed throughout the room. Raymond flinched, but he kept hold of the chair and ran for the kitchen doorway. Tesha grabbed another of the empty chairs and followed.

The first skeleton started to stand up. Raymond swung his chair as hard as he could and smashed it into the skull and shoulders. Bones flew all over the room. The two child skeletons started to get up and with only a moment's hesitation, Tesha smashed her chair into them as Raymond had done. They shattered completely, bones flying everywhere. The presumably mother skeleton stayed seated, turning her skull one way and the other to look at her decimated family. Tesha could almost feel sorry for her, but there was no time for sentiment.

Tesha stayed right behind Raymond though the kitchen. The moment they cleared the doorway, knives punctured the embroidered seat of Raymond's chair, slicing through the flimsy wood base. Luckily they stuck there, apparently unable to reverse out of the splintered wood. Pans flew at Tesha. She blocked them with her chair, holding it with legs pointed outwards. The impact of the heavier pans on chair legs threw off her balance and slowed her progress, but she forced her feet to keep moving forward, staying close behind Raymond so that much of the impact of items flying through the room at them was absorbed by his strong shoulders.

Though time seemed to stand still while they fought off the volatile kitchen implements, it actually took only a few seconds to press their way through the kitchen and through another doorway that led them into another corridor. This one had stairs.

Raymond turned and stepped behind Tesha as they cleared the doorway from the kitchen. He brought up his chair just in time to sideswipe an antique three-pronged toasting fork that he had seen whizzing straight towards her. The fork fell sideways, but immediately turned with tines pointed towards Raymond.

"Up the stairs!" he shouted. Raymond threw the chair so that it collided with the fork hurtling towards him. Like the knives, it pierced the seat of the chair, but the thicker implement shattered more of the wood and started quivering to pull itself out. Raymond sped towards the stairs. Tesha hesitated a moment at the bottom, unwilling to abandon Raymond to the vicious kitchen equipment. He leapt past her and took the stairs two at a time. Tesha followed close behind him, trying her best to see the edges of the steps from the inadequate swinging beam of light in front of Raymond.

They got as far as the middle of what had looked like an ordinary staircase, when the flat surfaces of the steps began to glow and to drift apart, turning at odd angles. Tesha had to focus all of her attention on placing her foot on each step, going by feel as much as by sight.

Suddenly she couldn't see the next step. One moment it was there, then it slid sideways and disappeared. The step after it was too high for her.

"Raymond!" she called, a hint of panic in her voice.

Raymond turned and saw her predicament. He had got a couple of steps ahead, but came back down to the step above what was now a growing gap. The lower steps appeared to be sinking into the floor.

"Take my hand!" he called. He crouched as far as he could

and reached towards Tesha. In that moment, he resembled his brother so strongly that Tesha could almost believe that it was Phillip who reached out to save her.

"Jump!" Raymond ordered as their hands clasped.

Tesha obeyed, leaping off the last step, though she knew she could never make it to the next one on her own. Raymond's strong arm pulled her across the gap and one foot landed on the lowest step where he had braced himself. The other leg dangled and it took an extra effort to pull it up from the gravity that tried to pull her downwards into the complete blackness between the two stairs. Even then Tesha might have toppled off if Raymond hadn't held fast to her, using his own weight to counterbalance her unsteadiness.

There was no time to ruminate on the situation. The stairs above them looked as if they were breaking up, shifting left and right like the lower stairs had done. Raymond leapt up two steps at a time again, holding Tesha's hand this time and pulling her up after him. When they reached the top, they found themselves on what looked like an ordinary landing. A wide hallway to the left led to several doors, presumably bedrooms. The ordinariness of the second floor landing felt deceptive, as if something new would happen to disorient reality in some way at any moment.

Tesha turned suddenly, a gasp escaping her lips. She had feared the kitchen implements might follow them up the stairs, but when she and Raymond looked down the staircase, all they saw were ordinary steps in place where they should have been.

"Was it all an illusion?" Tesha asked aloud.

That's some effective illusion," Raymond grumbled. "I could feel a hot wind coming from that gap in the stairs."

They turned at the same time to look back down the hall. Raymond directed his flashlight at the empty walls and at each of the

126

doors. There were four in all, two on each side.

Tesha squinted her eyes as the light beam passed what looked like some sort of marking on the wall.

"Bring the light closer," she said, stepping closer to see better. "I can see something here."

Raymond directed the light where she indicated.

"I don't see anything." He looked closely, trying to see what Tesha pointed at.

"It's really faint against the yellowed wallpaper. Like an orange discoloration."

"You forget, Tesha, I'm colorblind."

Tesha's head whirled round to look at Raymond.

"Sorry. I *did* forget. It's some kind of weird symbol. Not writing like downstairs in the dining room. How come you could see that?"

"Because the writing was a lot darker than the background."

Raymond shifted his shoulders slightly as if something suddenly made him feel uncomfortable.

"You were right, Tesha. Coming here tonight was a really stupid idea."

Tesha couldn't believe the sincerity she heard in Raymond's voice. This was a new side of her best friend's brother she had never seen. She wiped some tears from her cheeks, hoping he wouldn't notice the gesture in the dark. Thoughts of Phillip while his brother was saving her on the stairs had made them overflow.

"You couldn't have known things would get this crazy."

Tesha shook her head. "Nobody could have known. I just wonder... does anyone ever get out to tell others? Have other people got lost in here through history and just never been heard from again?"

She could only just see Raymond's shrug in the dim light.

"Who would know? People go missing all the time. Kids run away. Any of them could have come into this house and disappeared. Anyone who comes here makes sure no one sees them."

"They should bulldoze the place," Tesha remarked with a hint of anger. "If we get out, we have to go to Mayor Renick. We're two witnesses so he can't write either of us off as just crazy."

"Dylan or Ava might have got out already too," Raymond suggested. "I don't think the mayor would believe the kind of stuff we've seen if either of them told him what they saw, but at least if they told someone we're in here, they might send someone in to try to find us."

"Just what we need," Tesha chuffed. "A bunch of lost cops."

Raymond smiled.

"Not a bunch. Remember this town only has two."

Tesha gave a quick laugh, her hand flying to her mouth to quell the incongruous sound.

"Well," she said after a deep breath. "Which room should we try first?"

Raymond flashed his light over each of the doors again.

"Right now I wish we had Ava and her magic amulet to maybe use like a pendulum. At this point I'd take any help we can get."

Chapter Sixteen

Williamson steeled himself and opened the door as slowly and carefully as he could. When he shone the light in, he could see the dining table like before, only two chairs were missing now. The display cabinet they had moved was also gone without a trace, though the space where it once sat was easy to make out.

Williamson started to move through the door, then stopped and turned to Joseph.

"Come and hold this door open instead."

Joseph took one final look outside, then deliberately opened the front door as far as it would go before striding over to lean against the door to the next room. He glanced inside, seeing what Williamson had seen, though he didn't know about the display cabinet and only saw a space with a darker floor where something had apparently been moved.

Williamson looked suspiciously at the doorway to the kitchen. He crept up to the opening as if something might jump out at him and stayed behind the wall as much as possible while he shone his flashlight into the room to see what could be found. The missing dining room chairs were on the floor, slightly broken up and one of them with several large kitchen knives and the tines of an old toasting fork stuck through the wood of the seat underside.

This piqued his curiosity. Williamson risked a closer look around the wall, until he saw the knives quiver as if they were trying to free themselves. He quickly dropped the light beam to the floor behind him and moved away from the doorway. He began padding towards the door at the other end of the room, all but tiptoeing.

"Why are we being so quiet?" Joseph asked. "Shouldn't we be calling out to find our friends?"

Williamson's shoulders dropped.

"You're right," he conceded. "What's your friend's name? If there's a hallway behind that other door, I'll call for him. I haven't been farther than here. Just keep that door open, no matter what!"

"Raymond," Joseph informed the man. He turned and looked at the front door, expecting to find it still open. It was shut, though neither of them had heard it close. "If he don't answer, I say we get out and go get the police to help us."

As much as Williamson didn't like dealing with the police, he silently agreed with Joseph. He took a deep breath as he opened the other door, intending to bellow out Raymond's name. Instead, the grisly sight revealed by his flashlight made the bellow come out as a blood-curdling, high-pitched scream.

Father Michael expected to have to use the holy water to get the back door to open, like before. To his surprise, it began to open on its own as he and the Bishop approached. What was most eerie was the absolute silence. No tormented voices, no moans, not even the squeak of the hinges as the door slowly opened without any noise whatsoever. It was as if a void in the universe had sucked all sound out of the aethyr, leaving the priests in a world familiar only to the completely deaf.

The Bishop nodded to Father Michael, indicating that he should begin. Father Michael had expected the Bishop to lead the rite and wondered again what experience the older man had of exorcisms without actually having trained as an exorcist, but if the Bishop wanted him to initiate the rite, it was not Father Michael's place to question.

Father Michael began the litany once again in the original Latin.

"Exorcizamus te, omnis immunde spiritus, omni satanica potestas, omnis incursio infernalis adversarii, omnis legio, omnis congregatio et secta diabolica, in nomini et virtute Domini nostri Jesu Christi, eradicare et effugare a Dei Ecclesia, ab animabus ad imaginem Dei conditis ac pretioso divini Agni sanguini redemptis."

The Bishop echoed the passage after him in English translation.

"We cast you out, every unclean spirit, every satanic power, every onslaught of the infernal adversary, every legion, every diabolical group and sect, in the name and by the power of our Lord Jesus Christ. We command you, be gone and fly far from the Church of God, from the souls made by God in His image and redeemed by the precious blood of the divine Lamb."

They had walked up onto the back porch and Father Michael splashed some holy water inside the doorway. As he did so, he detected movement in his peripheral vision. While he was sprinkling the holy water, he shifted his gaze to either side of the doorway and had to struggle to suppress a natural reaction to flee. The dead rose vines had begun undulating as if they were live snakes, responding with hisses to his ministrations.

Instinctively, Father Michael threw some holy water over the slithering vines. A tortured scream echoed through his mind, though the vines made no audible sound. They moved away from the priest and Father Michael prepared to continue the rite. However, his mind suddenly went blank. He couldn't remember the Latin words! Father Michael turned to the Bishop, his confused expression showing that he was completely at a loss.

The Bishop, recognizing the priest's distress, poured some of his own holy water into his hand and sprinkled it over Father Michael's head, then he made the symbol of the cross on Father Michael's forehead and torso while speaking the most basic blessing.

"In the name of the Father, the Son, and the Holy Spirit, Amen."

Almost instantly, the words came tumbling out of Father Michael's mouth.

"Crux sacra sit mihi lux! Nunquam draco sit mihi dux. Vade retro Satana! Nunquam suade mihi vana! Sunt mala quae libas. Ipse venena bibas!"

Again, the Bishop followed with the translation.

"May the holy cross be my light! May the dragon never be my guide. Be gone Satan! Never tempt me with your vanities! What you offer me is evil. Drink the poison yourself!"

Father Michael glanced inside the doorway, tensed for the cupboards to start bleeding again. Nothing felt different. The rose vines and the doors had responded to holy water, but the presence that exuded from the house radiated an odious malevolence that showed no inclination to remove itself from the property.

He saw nothing out of the ordinary, but a whoosh of warm

air blew into his face from an open doorway at the back of the kitchen. It felt very like what he had experienced in the front room of the house when the demon had flapped its leathery wings.

Father Michael turned to the Bishop again. He could feel his entire body shaking. He knew his faith should keep him strong, but he couldn't stop the primal fear that threatened to overcome him. Still, he ignored his human weakness. He turned towards the kitchen and opened his mouth to begin the Latin prayers again, when the night was pierced by an almighty scream that could only have come from a man.

The priest tensed to run towards the sound, but the Bishop grasped his arm, preventing him from entering the house.

"We will go to the front. The scream sounded from that side of the house!"

Father Michael nodded and followed the Bishop towards the side path that led to the front of the house.

Every muscle in Joseph's body tensed at the sound of Williamson's scream. It was all he could do to hold himself in front of the open door, though he wasn't sure whether he wanted to run to help the man or to bolt out of the front door to escape. Williamson dropped the beam of his flashlight, but not before Joseph caught a glimpse of what had frightened the man so.

The body of Jerry Applegate stared lifelessly from the shelf where cobwebs wrapped him as securely as a cocoon. Joseph felt his stomach lurch. Applegate had been a friend of his parents since the family had moved to the small town and had always treated himself and his sisters like extended family.

Before he could gather his emotions or thoughts, a deep laugh drew his attention to the dining table where a small, dark man wearing a long, black coat and a tall hat sat smoking two cigarettes at the same time. When he spoke, it was with the clipped, Cajun French accented patois Joseph associated with the Guédé spirits of New Orleans voodoo tales.

"You recognize your friend, Jerry, eh? Meybe you like to come with us, yes? We have a good time. Have a drink, we go find some women and taste the pleasures a man likes. You are young. You like rum and women, eh?"

Joseph looked at the entity with suspicion. Williamson stood aghast, as shocked by the sudden appearance of the strange little man as he had been by the discovery of the security guard's body. He took out a cigarette of his own and started to light it with a disposable lighter. After a moment, Joseph found his voice.

"You are not Loa!"

The entity frowned.

"Why you say that? When you stand on the crossroads..."

"This ain't no crossroads!" Joseph shrieked. "This house is in the middle of a block!"

The entity shook it's head from side to side, at the same time wagging a long finger as if to correct a pupil.

"Where once was death, always there is death. Come with me, young Joseph. Drink and be free of this painful life."

The entity held up a hip flask, offering it to Joseph, though it ignored Williamson who looked from one to the other, the flame of his lighter still dancing in the semi-darkness as he stood frozen, unsure what to say or do.

"I go nowhere with you!" Joseph bellowed as if the entity had angered him. He stepped towards the little man and watched him fade into a shadow of the room, still wagging his finger in remonstrance, until he disappeared completely.

Joseph turned towards Williamson, glancing at the door to the living room that had closed now that he had stepped away from it to confront the strange voodoo-like entity, then his eyes opened wide as a wave of blackness poured out of the cupboard behind Williamson, immersing his feet.

Williamson turned the flashlight downward to reveal that the wave was comprised of thousands of spiders. Big ones, little ones, mostly black though Joseph was sure he saw the earthy shade of brown recluse spiders among them. Williamson stumbled backwards a step, turning to look for an escape. His lighter caught on the cobwebs and they flared up like dry kindling.

Joseph saw that the spiders were flowing straight for him. He jumped onto a chair and sucked in a deep breath, then let out a scream so shrill that it brought back Williamson's memory of Joseph's promise to scream like a little girl.

Chapter Seventeen

Ava sipped the last of her tea, forcing herself not to make a sour face. It had gone cold while she explained everything that had happened at Number 23 Hazelwood Avenue that evening to her Aunt Laurie. She had held nothing back, but filled in all the details about the planning, the escape from the party, then the anomalies she had seen in the house, not least of all walking though a door and finding herself in a room on a different floor than she had previously been on. Ava and Laurie actually laughed together about Ava's less than graceful flight down the neighboring house's tree.

Laurie listened attentively until Ava came to the end of her story, then she nodded and led Ava back into the living room where she began to gather a few items out of various drawers and cupboards.

"Let's go then," Aunt Laurie said in her matter-of-fact way. She handed Ava a cloth bag with some of the items to carry and slung another over her own shoulder. Like everyone in town, Laurie already knew the way to Number 23 Hazelwood Avenue.

The walk was only a few blocks, but the night was chilly. Ava could see the vapour from her breath as soon as they stepped outside. Worse, she felt an internal resistance to going back to Hazelwood Avenue. It was only the thought of her brother still trapped in the house that gave her the courage to press on. She clutched the amulet Aunt Laurie had given her, sure that it held some sort of protective magic.

"Aunt Laurie, what is this stone?" she asked as they walked.

"Obsidian," Laurie answered at once. "It's a truth-enhancing, protective stone. It brings clarity to the mind and clears confusion. It also blocks psychic attack and absorbs negativity. It stimulates exploration into the unknown while offering protection, so you did exactly the right thing when you used it to find a way out of the house. Clever girl!"

"It just felt like the right thing to do!" Ava gave her aunt a beaming smile, delighted with the praise. Of all her cousins, Aunt Laurie had apparently singled Ava out as someone who could appreciate her knowledge of the esoteric.

"Will you teach me about other stones, please?"

Aunt Laurie smiled.

"Your parents would object if I started teaching you directly, but I'm sure I can guide you to a book or two that you would find useful."

The promise lightened Ava's mood and partially dispelled her fears, though the thought of what she had experienced at Number 23 Hazelwood Avenue still made her tremble. She couldn't help wondering if her mother had ever known anything of magic. She and Aunt Laurie were sisters, after all.

Aunt Laurie looked at Ava sideways, as if she could read her thoughts.

"Whatever happens tonight, you're not to go near that property ever again. Agreed?"

Ava readily agreed to that. If it weren't for Dylan, she would have nothing further to do with the place even now. She had been prepared to send the police to help find her other friends if Aunt Laurie hadn't been able to help. As they turned the corner onto Hazelwood Avenue, it occurred to Ava that she had no idea what Aunt Laurie planned to do. She clutched her obsidian amulet again, trusting to her aunt's magic.

Tesha and Raymond crept little by little down the upstairs hallway. Raymond kept the light moving, looking for anything that might jump out and surprise them. Tesha saw more of the mysterious markings along the walls, but she didn't draw Raymond's attention to them. Whatever they were, there was no point in giving him more to worry about.

They passed the first two doors, opposite each other in the hall. Neither of them wanted to suggest which one they should open. They couldn't stay in the hall forever, but any new room might bring new terrors and both of them had been through more than enough scares already, not to mention the grief that circumstances hadn't allowed them to fully process yet.

Tesha thought of Phillip falling through some unknown abyss and tears sprang to her eyes again. She wondered how Raymond was managing to keep it together after losing his brother.

When they came to the second pair of doors, they exchanged a brief glance.

"Which one? Left or right?" Raymond asked.

"Will it matter?" Tesha moaned. "If the house has something more planned for us, it will probably be behind whichever door we choose."

Tesha let her own words sink in. She was talking about a house as if it had an intelligence of its own. She knew it sounded crazy. The thought pressed her into a decision.

"Right," she blurted. "It's traditionally auspicious."

Raymond nodded, the dim light of his flashlight reflecting off the light yellowish-colored walls making his gesture visible, if only in silhouette.

Tesha stepped towards the right hand door with Raymond following close behind, shining his flashlight towards the edge where it would open. Tesha grasped the brass doorknob, squeezing tightly to try to stop her hand from shaking. Then she turned it and pushed the door open no more than an inch.

She peered into the gap, getting a first glimpse of the room with the help of Raymond's flashlight, then gingerly pushed the door open further.

Raymond's mouth dropped open. The room appeared to be an ordinary bedroom. The shapes of a bed and chest of drawers were clearly visible in the light shining in through two windows on the opposite wall.

"Windows!" Tesha gasped. Then her breath caught in an arrested yelp. Next to the right hand window, just visible in the shadows, an elderly woman sat in a stylish, red upholstered chair, gazing out of the window.

"I tried to warn them," she said with sadness in her soft voice. It was then that Tesha decided the woman wasn't so much elderly as worn, much as homeless people too often looked much older than their years from hardships unimaginable. The woman's head turned to regard her visitors.

"I have limited ability, as you see." She stood up and spread her hands. The fleur de lis pattern on the wallpaper was clearly visible through her ethereal body. Tesha noticed that her own mouth hung open like Raymond's and promptly shut it.

"Are you a g-gho..."

"A ghost?" the faded woman preempted. "No more than a shade of what I was. I can make the lights flash across the windows, but nothing more... substantial. You are safe here. You've seen the wards. The upstairs is closed to the foul influence downstairs."

Tesha remembered the symbols she had noted on the walls in the hallway. Raymond hadn't seen most of them, but he was more concerned with the anomalies they had experienced on the floor below.

"What *is* downstairs? A demon? I heard it laugh." It was the first Tesha knew that Raymond had heard that deep, sinister laugh too.

"Call it what you will," the ghostly woman replied. "It's the collective malice of all the wrongdoers who were hanged on this spot, back when it was the crossroads."

"Crossroads?" Tesha made no attempt to conceal her surprise. "I've never heard anything about hangings at a crossroads in this town. I thought this was one of the oldest streets..."

"So it is, my dear." The woman appeared to smile slightly. "The streets were re-laid intentionally that this spot would be forgotten. There may be records somewhere. I do not know."

"But..." Tesha thought a moment, unable to formulate her need to know into words, then she asked a different question instead.

"Who are you?"

Tesha thought the woman looked sad as she answered.

"I was one of the innocents. Hanged for a witch, though I never did anyone harm."

A moment passed in silence, then the woman spoke again.

"The couple who had the house built were innocents too, but they carried the transgressions of their forefathers in their blood."

Tesha bunched her brows in a quizzical expression and opened her mouth to speak, but the ghostly woman cut her off.

"You don't have much time. The first room on the left as you come up the stairs is the one you want. You must go quickly."

"But our friends..." Raymond began.

"The little girl got out," the woman told them. "The one who was taken by the pit... he is with *us* now."

Raymond hung his head.

"What of Dylan, Ava's brother?" Tesha looked at the woman hopefully.

"I will do my best to guide him out. Now you must go, at once!"

Raymond was the first to start moving. He tugged at Tesha's elbow, leading her back to the hallway. As soon as they stepped outside of the bedroom, they saw why the ghostly woman had urged them to hurry so vehemently. Smoke billowed up the stairs from a fire somewhere below.

"Come on!" Raymond sprinted toward the room the woman had told them to try. Tesha ran to catch up, though her instincts were to run away from the fire rather than towards the smoke filling the hallway. Raymond burst through the door of the other bedroom without caution.

To her relief, Tesha saw light shining through windows, just like in the bedroom with the ghost. More importantly, there were two walls with windows and the one to the left had the branches of a monkey puzzle tree pressed up against the glass. They had found the room at the front corner of the house!

Tesha didn't break stride. She shut the bedroom door to keep the smoke at bay and went straight to the window with the tree outside. The pane pushed up easily and she started to climb out, telling herself that climbing down would be easier than getting up the tree. Besides, there were plenty of branches to use as holds.

The sword cane still stuck in her belt caught on the window sill and she considered whether she should leave it behind.

She wouldn't need it now that they were getting out and her parents would never allow her to keep it, whether it was legal or not. Regret ached in her as she slid it out of her belt and laid it on a chest next to the window, then she climbed out, grabbing branches tightly while her feet searched for stability in the branches. They felt flimsy, even for her small weight.

Raymond followed Tesha, stuffing his flashlight into his belt and climbing deftly like his brother had so many times in Tesha's memory. Moving one arm or leg at a time while clinging and stepping carefully felt slow, but so far the smoke wasn't visible in the front of the house and there was no sign of actual flames.

Tesha got nearly low enough to jump the last few feet when she heard a hiss and instinctively retracted the leg that was about to step on a lower branch. A black snake struck the branch where her leg would have been, the same leg that had already suffered a bite from the Rakshasa.

"Snakes!" she shouted up to Raymond.

He reached for his flashlight and directed it towards the ground beneath them. The long grass was teaming with snakes slithering through the overgrown blades. Tesha recognized the distinctive diamond pattern of rattlesnakes and could now hear their warning rattles. She also noted a brown-patterned copperhead and one reddish species. Unnatural though it was, the different varieties of poisonous snakes writhed together, hissing and spitting upwards at the escapees in the tree.

"The sword!" Raymond yelled. He started climbing back upwards, but had only gone three or four branches up when one he grabbed onto snapped.

Tesha screamed, watched helplessly as Raymond fell between the branches, plummeting towards the ground and the swarm of venomous snakes.

Chapter Eighteen

Father Michael and the Bishop slammed into the front door, locked against them once more, at the same moment that a higher pitched scream split the night. Father Michael splashed the last of his holy water onto the door, but it held fast.

"Allow me," the Bishop proposed. He took a small vial from his cassock pocket and dotted drops of the contents onto the door into the form of a cross as he prayed the *Our Father* in Latin.

"Pater noster, qui es in caelis, sanctificetur nomen tuum. Adveniat regnum tuum. Fiat voluntas tua, sicut in caelo et in terra. Panem nostrum quotidianum da nobis hodie, et dimitte nobis debita nostra sicut et nos dimittimus debitoribus nostris. Et ne nos inducas in tentationem, sed libera nos a malo. Amen."

Then suddenly he shouted a command.

"INTROITU SINERET ASHTAROTH!"

The door creaked open no more than an inch. The Bishop rushed it, as if he were afraid it would slam in his face any moment. Without hesitation, the elderly man followed the sounds of continuous shrill screaming to a door on the opposite wall. This one didn't resist him. He burst through, closely followed by Father Michael, to see a young man, still screaming and dancing around on a heavy oak dining table, squashing spiders as they climbed over the edges. Another man was feebly attempting to stop both the flow of spiders and a growing fire from encroaching through an open door in the right hand corner of the room, but the spiders filled the doorway so that it wouldn't close.

Williamson turned at the sound of the Bishop's body slamming through the door and leapt towards the priest. Father Michael recognized the man who had warned him against this house in Mayor Renick's office.

"Don't let that door shut!" Williamson screamed in panic. He turned to Joseph, still battling the spider hoard on the table. "Come on!"

Joseph saw the chance for escape and leaped from the table in a long jump that would win an Olympic championship right through the doorway and into the living room. The priests and Williamson followed, slamming the door behind them. Joseph reached the front door first, but it had closed again and the knob refused to turn. Black smoke was beginning to seep under the door from the dining room.

"My friends may still be in the house!" Joseph burbled in panic. "We have to get them out before the whole place goes up!"

The bishop turned to him.

"Do you know positively they are here...?" He left the last word dangling, inviting the boy to fill in a name.

"Joseph," the panicking youth supplied. "Joseph Despre. They must be here! They never came back to the party!"

"Could they have gone home?" Williamson suggested. "Maybe if they got scared..."

"Or met with the security guard and were sent on their way,"

Father Michael offered. "We met at the mayor's office, didn't we?"

Williamson nodded.

"The security guard is dead," Williamson informed the priest. "His body was in that cupboard, with the fire."

Father Michael and the Bishop exchanged an apprehensive glance. The Bishop turned to Joseph and spoke kindly to him.

"We have to trust that they've escaped, or will when the fire diminishes the demon's power. We cannot go through the fire ourselves. We must trust to God for their safety."

The light from the streetlights shining through the window suddenly dimmed, leaving the small group in darkness. Williamson turned on his flashlight, wondering when it had turned off. He could see nothing beyond arms reach ahead of himself. A familiar deep, sinister laugh reverberated around the walls, just as Father Michael remembered from his previous experience inside the house. Williamson also remembered that bone-chilling sound and felt his bladder release.

"Elliot!" a rasping, low voice intoned as if summoning an age-old cohort. *"We have missed you."*

The Bishop looked at once uncomfortable. Father Michael raised his eyebrows in question, but the Bishop could not see the gesture in the darkness.

"That name was left behind me when I took the cloth. You have no claim on me, Ashtaroth!"

A shadow of large leathery wings, black against black, became discernable within the darkness. A whoosh of warm air flowed into the faces of the trapped men as the wings moved ponderously forward.

"What in Hell is that?" Joseph asked incredulously. "Some kind of Apocalyptic super demon? Sorry Fathers..."

"You needn't apologize," the Bishop assured him. "You assess His origin correctly. A Duke of Hell, sometimes confused in mythology with an ancient Pagan goddess, is what holds possession of this cursed house."

"It s-sounds like you've met before," Williamson stuttered. He didn't bother trying to hide his abject terror.

The Bishop's reply sounded as if it were laced with regret.

"We all have pasts. In my youth I studied a book called the *De praestigiis daemonum* and other tomes of occult lore. My youthful folly is... regrettable."

Williamson took his crucifix necklace out and held the cross in his hand as he muttered the only prayer he knew.

"Our Father who art in heaven, hallowed be thy name. Thy kingdom come, thy will be done on earth as it is in heaven..." It was all he knew of the common prayer. He repeated the few lines over and over again, his eyes wide with terror.

The demon became gradually more visible and Father Michael found himself studying its form. He had expected something more goat-like, but the shape that he began to make out as his eyes adjusted looked more like an orc from the *Lord of the Rings* movies with a basically deformed humanoid visage, only with wings. Rather than hooves as he might have expected, it had long feet with at least four-inch talons at the ends of what looked like six toes.

All the while Joseph kept swiveling his head, looking first towards the demon, then at the dark patch where he had seen the door to freedom beckoning before the light muted, then back at the growing cloud of black smoke filling the back of the room. Like the demon, the minimal illumination made it appear black against black. He shivered, wondering if the spiders might also be crawling in under the door, invisible in the darkness. The sound of fire crackling in the next room gave him hope that at least the crawling things might have perished in the flames.

"We got to get outta here," he urged. "This whole place is going up!"

"With the destruction of the house," the Bishop predicted, "the tormented spirits who give the demon his power will be dispersed."

Joseph looked at the Bishop aghast, unsure whether the priest expected them to all give up and die for the sake of stopping the evil of this place.

The demon's laugh echoed around the walls again, surrounding the helpless group of men. Father Michael felt the hairs on the back of his neck stand up.

"You shall perish for your trespass," the rasping voice boasted. "But the spirits who have power over this place under my command will not so easily be disseminated."

Father Michael began to intone the rite of exorcism in Latin once more.

"Exorcizamus te, omnis immunde spiritus, omni satanica potestas, omnis incursio infernalis adversarii..."

The Bishop joined in and took the small vial from his pocket he had used before. He began sprinkling the contents in the direction of the demon blocking the door.

"I smell sulphur!" Joseph exclaimed. He began clapping and foot stomping, creating a rhythm, then he started a counterpoint to the priests' prayers in a sort of sing-song intonation.

"You, Grand Bois, You, Carrafour, You, Baron Cemetiere, You, Damballah, In your all powerful names I have invoked with this offering, I command evil demons and hexes to flee this dwelling, never to return!"

The silhouette of the demon turned sharply first one way then another with its arms held out from its body, giving the impression of immense agitation. It cowered from the substance in the little bottle, much to Father Michael's confusion. The salted holy water he had used had seemed to lose its effectiveness, but whatever the Bishop had thrown at the entity made it dissipate into the darkness. The light from the street slowly brought visibility back and with it, clear sight of the door.

Joseph danced over to the door to freedom, still singing, and grasped the doorknob. The last words of his song came out in a sigh of relief. The doorknob turned.

Chapter Nineteen

Ava and Laurie arrived at Number 23 Hazelwood Avenue to see Raymond and Tesha climbing down the monkey puzzle tree in front of the house. Ava started to breathe a sigh of relief, then Raymond slipped and Tesha screamed. A small cry escaped Ava's lips in response, but Raymond caught himself, grabbing onto one of the plentiful branches close to where Tesha held herself onto the lower branches.

Aunt Laurie wasted no time. She dropped her shoulder bag onto the pavement and began taking out various items. Ava dropped her bag next to the other one and watched with some confusion as her aunt pulled out two wet towels, which she twisted together into some sort of symbol and left on the ground.

Laurie next produced a glass bowl, into which she poured some water from a bottle, a small jar which Ava had seen on display at Aunt Laurie's house and knew contained salt, a smudging stick, made of sage, an essential oil bottle and a blue candle held within a glass fishbowl. She also took out a box of wooden matches and lit the blue candle, reaching her fingers inside the fishbowl to keep the wind from blowing it out.

Laurie spread a drop of oil from the small bottle onto the smudge stick, then took a pinch of salt from the jar and sprinkled it across the water she had poured into the glass bowl, releasing it slowly while moving her hand in a pentagram pattern. She began to chant.

"By the purifying power of water, the clean breath of air, the dynamism of fire, and the grounding energy of earth, we cleanse this place and repel all evil and negativity, so mote it be."

Just as Laurie came to the end of the chant, two priests came running out of the front door, followed by black, billowing smoke. Two other figures emerged from the smoke behind them, coughing and sucking in air as they cleared the door.

The last one out had the presence of mind to shut the door and as the smoke cleared, Ava could see that it was Raymond's friend, Joseph. Tesha and Raymond's struggle on the monkey puzzle tree diverted their immediate attention. Ava expected the men to help her friends, but they ran to the edge of the porch and abruptly stopped, looking down at the overgrown lawn.

That was when Ava noticed the unusual movement in the long grass. She opened her mouth to tell Aunt Laurie, but her aunt was already muttering words in a cadence that sounded like another spell and she held a finger to her lips, indicating that Ava wasn't to interrupt.

She pointed at the edge of the lawn closest to them and Ava could see why Tesha and Raymond weren't climbing the rest of the way down from the tree or the others going to their aid. Snakes slithered among the blades of grass. Too many different species in close proximity to be natural. Ava heard the distinctive rattle of a rattlesnake and took a step backwards away from the long grass.

Father Michael wondered at the sudden dissipation of the demon's power as they pushed through the door. Was there something in the Bishop's holy water that was different than his own? Or had whatever ritual dance Joseph had performed had some effect?

Whatever the reason, they had escaped the burning building and Joseph had the good sense to close the front door against the billowing smoke. Father Michael took a deep breath of fresh air and was about to ask the young man about the strange performance, when Joseph shouted in the direction of a tree in front of the house.

"Raymond! Tesha! What you doin' up there?"

He moved towards the edge of the porch with the other men whose attention had been alerted to the young people in the tree when Tesha cried out.

"Don't step in the grass! Snakes!"

Joseph looked down to see she was right. What must have been hundreds of snakes teaming through the unkempt ground cover writhed together, hissing and spitting like something out of an Indiana Jones movie.

"How do we get out of here?" he cried, not expecting an answer.

"Who's that?" Williamson shouted, pointing to a woman and a teenage girl just beyond the grass on the pavement. The woman had lit a clump of something and was beginning to wave it towards the grass and presumably more snakes. At that moment, the sound of voices singing an old hymn echoed down the street and a horde of people appeared from the corner of Hazelwood Avenue, led by old Mrs. Elwin. Father Michael counted nine people in the small mob.

"Shall we gather at the riiiiver! Where bright angel feet have trod!" the voices sang.

The Bishop actually covered his face with the palm of his hand.

"God save us from his devout followers," he muttered so softly that only Father Michael could hear him.

～

Delilah Elwin prided herself on having been a God-fearing woman all her life, but when she had joined the West Parrish Church of the Holy Baptism, she had discovered a pro-active community for doing the Lord's work. Together they had picketed abortion clinics, disrupted funerals for lefties, commies and fags and voted for that president who hated everyone the Lord hates.

It was a shame about him losing his impeachment appeal and shooting all those people, but Mrs. Elwin knew that it was all because he was trying to do the right thing. That a president of these United States should end his days in a hospital for the criminally insane was just undignified!

Why the church's minister hadn't taken action against that devil-spawned house in their town before now she couldn't fathom, but with *Catholics* performing their heathen rituals in plain sight of the street, she could see that it was time her devout brethren made their presence known.

Getting people out in the middle of the night, and devil's night to boot, hadn't been easy. The minister himself had pleaded a sick child and refused to come. But as secretary of the church she had the phone numbers for the whole congregation and eight servants of the Lord had dragged themselves out of bed to join her in doing His work.

As they approached the house known as Number 23 Hazelwood Avenue, Mrs. Elwin could see two of those heathen priests cavorting on the front porch with another man and a young black man. Mrs. Elwin frowned over the mixing of races. If they had to have minorities in their town at all, they should at least stick to

153

their own.

As if Catholics weren't bad enough, a young girl in a witch dress and pointed hat was helping some hippy-looking woman with what could only be witchcraft, with her candle and chanting as bold as brass right there on the street! No doubt they were doing some sort of evil magic to trap the two people in the tree, unless they were there to break into the house and look for antique valuables.

Then Mrs. Elwin caught the reflection of a street lamp on the face of the girl in the tree and saw she was another minority, probably a Muslim by the look of her.

Pagans, heathens, Catholics and all, Satan had to be driven out of that house once and for all before it attracted any more undesirables to this street. The congregation continued to sing as she sniffed derisively and stepped towards the tall grass at a point where she remembered seeing a paved path in days when it wasn't so overgrown.

Just as she was about to set foot on the lawn, Mrs. Elwin was startled by a hiss and rattling sound. She recoiled and looked closer at the grass to see that it concealed a host of poisonous snakes. Her eyes opened wide and she nearly screamed, then she remembered herself, that she was leading this flock tonight and must appear to be in complete control. She pointed at the writhing reptiles and Brother George, one of the congregation who had boasted of handling snakes in another church where faith was tested by entering a snake pit, moved forward.

George's faith was such that he didn't hesitate. He continued singing as he took a confident step into the wriggling mass.

"Yes, we'll gather at the river! The beautiful, the beautiful river; Gather with the saints at the river, That flows by the throne of God!"

The first strike came quickly. A collective gasp from the other members of the church group stopped the song. Three more snake strikes in fast succession knocked George off balance and he stumbled, nearly falling into the writing mass surrounding him.

⌒⌒⌒

While the churchy people acted like idiots, Aunt Laurie set her smudge stick alight and got a good smoke cloud going. She turned to Ava and instructed her to hold her amulet and think about how she had felt when she had used it to find a door to a room where she could escape the house. Now she was to focus on parting the snakes so that the people trapped in front of the house could get away.

Aunt Laurie gave her a chant to say over and over again, but instructed Ava that she was not to set foot within the grass, no matter what. Then she held the smudge stick at grass level and recited the same repeating chant in time with Ava.

Laurie grabbed the collar of the ridiculous man as he was about to fall among the biting snakes and threw him with surprising strength towards the relative safety of the pavement. He landed face first and one of the others helped him to stumble away, presumably to get medical help for the bites and whatever venom had been injected into his bloodstream.

Ava did as her aunt told her, even when the church members tried to interrupt her chant and jibed her for practicing witchcraft. One of the 'faithful' even shoved her shoulder to try to knock her over. There were no thanks forthcoming for her aunt's intervention that saved one of their members, but instead some of the group shouted "Praise the Lord for Brother George's deliverance!" and other pat phrases to shift credit for his salvation to their deity.

Laurie took one cautious step after another, forging a path

through the long, undulating grass. Whether it was the smoke itself or something in the magic, the slithering things moved away from her and the grass itself appeared to part before her steps.

She could see the Bishop on the porch sprinkling holy water into the lethal sea of reptiles, achieving at least partial success. The priests had managed to cut a path to the tree and were helping the teenagers down with the boy who had come out of the house with them sticking close behind them. The man who had also been with them paced back and forth on the porch in an agitated manner, apparently too fearful to trust to faith, magic or anything that would put him among the snakes.

Laurie felt she had no choice but to direct her path towards the larger group.

Williamson knew it made sense to stick close to the priests. The holy water was working. The snakes were clearing a path, but he could see how little water was left in the bottle and there was no chance it would hold out enough to get past the entire lawn. He could see a woman out by the street waving something that gave off smoke that appeared to be forging a path in front of her, but there was no way of knowing how long her incendiary would burn or whether it would continue to be effective.

Joseph had been the smart one. He had stuck as close to the priests as a shadow, safe within their protected sphere. Williamson paced back and forth on the porch like a caged animal, constrained by a primal fear of slithering reptiles. He clenched his fists in anger, mostly at himself for his cowardice. Williamson knew he should follow the priests before it was too late. Already the snakes were beginning to fill in the furrow in the grass left by the priests and Joseph pushing their way through, though the creatures avoided the wet blades.

No one even appeared to notice that he had been left behind, abandoned, while they put their efforts into rescuing the teenagers. He could smell the smoke from the fire in the house, not yet visible but undoubtedly seeping under the door. The whole place could go up at any moment. He would have to ignore his apprehension and just jump before the only chance at escape filled in with writhing snakes!

Williamson made one more circuit back and forth, his fists clenching and unclenching while his feet stomped on the wood porch, keeping time with the sound of his heartbeat thumping in his ears. Then he turned and ran the last lap across the porch, leaping off the edge towards the forged path.

He landed right on target, his feet coming down where the grass blades parted left and right and the snakes pulled back as if the ground itself burned them. Unfortunately he landed too hard. Williamson heard his ankle snap before he felt the pain. He screamed as the broken ankle failed him and he fell sideways... right into the snake-infested grass.

The sound of the girl's scream echoing his own was the last thing he heard in the world he once knew. Williamson's body hadn't even hit the ground before the first bites landed on his arms and face. The sharp pains covered his body in seconds. The only things he could hear were the rattles and hisses from the reptiles surrounding him, those who hadn't yet sunk their venomous fangs into his tortured flesh. His consciousness wavered. Somewhere on a discarnate level, he became aware of a sharp pain, deep within his chest.

His final moment came in silence. He tried to open his eyes, but could only manage slits because his face was swollen in countless places. A larger snake than all the others appeared from the lowest point of concealment within the ground cover. Williamson's only thought was of the Tarzan episodes he had watched as a child. He knew what a constrictor looked like. The massive boa dropped its jaw, opening its mouth wide. Williamson felt the smooth flesh of the snake's insides as they slipped around his head and shoulders, much like a reverse birthing experience. Then he knew no more.

⁓

Tesha was on the ground, though far from safe. Her eyes were wide as she watched the waves of undulating grass bend away from the places where the older priest threw his holy water. Raymond had caught a branch to halt his fall, but his legs were left dangling just above their rescuers. The younger priest and Joseph each took a leg and guided it towards a branch where Raymond could gain a foothold, then kept hands available to grasp for balance while he found the rest of the way down.

A man's scream from the direction of the porch seized their attention. Tesha screamed in response as she turned and saw the man fall into the ocean of snakes. Waves of the deadly creatures spiraled in towards where he had disappeared like the froth of a shark feeding frenzy on the surface of the ocean. A heartbeat later, a sudden explosion shook the house, shattering glass from the windows as flames leaped out to light the sky in ominous shadows, just as the town clock began chiming midnight. The snakes fled, streaming away from the house as if guided by a collective mind.

Raymond took his final jump down from the tree, urged on by the immediate peril of falling glass and growing flames. The fire roared with a deafening fury that transformed into a bestial wail with a reverberating metallic screech. A black form rose above the roof of the house, it's features indistinct apart from what appeared to be horns and two appendages that might have been arms or tentacles. Beneath the noise of this almighty howl and the last chimes of the clock tower, Tesha and Raymond heard a softer cry, one that was recognizably human.

158

"Dylan!" they shouted together. Raymond followed the sound to the left, lower corner of the house. He ripped aside handfuls of overgrown grass and found a narrow basement window at ground level. It was open and Dylan was inside, trying to climb up to get enough purchase to climb through. Raymond could see the basement was filling with smoke. He grasped both Dylan's arms and pulled, using one foot to push against the side of the house for leverage. He wasn't strong enough to pull him up as dead weight. Dylan's wrists started to slip from his hands, though Raymond gripped them as hard as he could.

Just when Raymond was sure he was going to lose him, the priests grabbed an arm each and leaned backwards, using their weight to help pull while Joseph grabbed Raymond by the waist and heaved as well. Dylan found his footing and pushed from inside. Suddenly he was out.

No words were necessary. With smoke pouring out of the house now and the snakes fleeing, all of them ignored the slithering things and ran for the street.

When the house exploded into flames and the nearest snakes started slithering onto the pavement, Ava jumped up onto one of the black cars parked behind her that had a crucifix hanging from the mirror. The tsunami of slithering reptiles that followed sent what was left of the 'faithful' running and screaming into the night, except Mrs. Elwin who stood her ground, shouting at the escaping serpents of evil and verbally smiting them in the Lord's name.

She didn't notice the copperhead who smelt water and found its way under the hedge of the house across the street and into the welcoming pond, bountifully stocked with fish.

Aunt Laurie stopped halfway across the lawn, watching the

flow of elongated vertebrates parting around her cloud of sage smoke, streaming off in all directions. They were followed by the priests and the teenagers she had come to find, strolling casually behind the swell of reptilians flowing through the long grass.

Sirens blared in the distance. She breathed a sigh of relief that someone had thought to call the fire department. Probably one of the neighbors worried about their own properties.

Laurie overheard the younger priest talking to the dark-skinned young man.

"What was that clapping and dancing all about you did in the house just before the demon disappeared?"

Joseph had breathed in some of the smoke and coughed for a few seconds before he could speak.

"My grandmama taught me that. Old New Orleans protection spell against negative energies."

"Voodoo?"

"Not all Voodoo is stickin' pins in dolls. In New Orleans, a lot of the voodoo stuff is for the tourists, but even the most devout Christians got a bit of old magic in their souls. As soon as I smelt the sulphur, I remembered what grandmama told me. She's first generation from Haiti and the old magic's still strong there."

"Dylan!" Ava shouted. She slid down from the car and ran up to her brother, stopping just short of giving him a hug. "Can we go home now? I don't want to stay at Amy's anymore."

Dylan opened his mouth to reply, but his eyes were wide. Raymond thought he looked shell-shocked, not that he'd ever seen anyone after an actual war. This night had been traumatic enough.

"Take your sister home, Dylan," he advised. "I'll come over

tomorrow and we can talk."

Joseph turned and caught up with Raymond, giving him a high-five. A fire engine and a police car came around the corner, lights flashing and sirens piercing the night. Tesha, Raymond, Joseph, Dylan and Ava began walking in the other direction, disappearing into the shadows and leaving Mrs. Elwin still ranting at the demons inside her mind.

Tesha overheard the priests talking as the group of teenagers passed them, discussing what report they would make to the mayor the following day. She cringed. They might walk away unnoticed now, but the loss of Phillip would have to be explained to his parents and probably the police as well. For now, she just wanted to be far away from Number 23 Hazelwood Avenue.

The last words she heard from the priests before they were too far to hear was the younger one asking the Bishop what was in his holy water that smelled of sulphur and whether his extra ingredients should be made known to the exorcists of the church. The Bishop's answer perplexed Tesha.

"Some substances, despite their power, require harvesting methods unsuitable to widespread use in the church. It is best we let this matter lie."

Chapter Twenty

Tesha's sister Aarya tried to catch snowflakes with her tongue as the sisters walked at a solemn pace. The blowey November flurry portended winter settling in at last. Tesha carried a large bouquet of flowers, bought at the florist since fresh flowers were out of season.

"I think you were really lucky, not getting grounded. Even if it did take them almost a month to decide!" Aarya had always been outspoken. Tesha was just glad to have her sister's company for a little while when the rambunctious girl might have had other things to do on a Sunday.

"Mom and Dad understood my reason for disobeying them, that I went because I thought Ava might need protection. I won't hold my breath on ever being allowed to go to another all night party again though." Tesha leaned the flowers on her left arm and pushed a lock of hair out of her eyes, using the motion to wipe a tear that had escaped down her cheek. "They let me off easy, but that's partly because I lost my best friend."

Aarya pretended not to notice her older sister's eyes brimming over with more tears.

"Is Raymond coming over today? Maybe he can be your best friend now."

Tesha smiled at her sister's innocent child logic.

"Raymond looks a lot like Phillip, but they are very different people. We're friends of sorts, but he's only been around because we've been working on some local research. It's finished now."

Finding historical information on the town from before the streets were re-laid had not been easy. Once Joseph and Raymond had compared experiences, learning that Joseph had been told by some form of ethereal entity that the house was on a site that was once a crossroads, just like the ghostly woman on the upper floor had told Tesha and Raymond, the three of them had started digging for information.

The Internet had nothing to offer. Joseph and Raymond did manual research, first in town records, then at the library at the state capital, until they found an old ordinance map and a newspaper story about the couple who had been found slaughtered in the house. Apparently the wife had been a direct descendant of the hangman who had presided over the majority of executions that had occurred on the site.

The boys had brought their findings to Tesha to co-ordinate into a full story. Despite the fact that she hadn't actually been grounded, Tesha had effectively been under house arrest for over three weeks while her parents hedged about whether she deserved punishment under the circumstances. She hadn't gone anywhere for the entire month of November except to school and to the police station to make a statement.

There were many things Tesha wasn't ready to tell her younger sister. Raymond could never be her confidante like Phillip had been. She felt bereft of her best friend now more than ever. She wished so hard that Phillip was here to tell him about the bite on her leg, how it kept getting worse and her worries about the blackened, festering skin that was slowly spreading across her calf. She knew she should tell her parents and go to a doctor, but she kept disinfecting the wound and hoping it would heal on its own.

Phillip would have enjoyed laughing over the tale of her excursion the morning after the incident to go back to the house at dawn to retrieve the antique sword cane. She had seen it fly out of the upstairs window when the house exploded. No one in the family had seen her sneak out. It was a secret she could share with no one now. She could only keep the antique hidden, keep it safe.

Then there was the confidence that Phillip had shared with her just before he died. Phillip's memorial service had been for family only. No one who attended would ever know that Phillip had been gay. Tesha thought it was a shame that such things would upset the family who purported to love him. None of them ever knew him as she did, not even his brother.

They reached the corner of Hazelwood Avenue and stopped. Silence had fallen between them while Tesha had been lost in her thoughts. Now it was Aarya who broke it.

"Are you sure you want to go by yourself? I don't even walk down this street anymore!"

"I feel like I have to," Tesha tried to explain. "I haven't looked at the memorial statue yet and as far as I'm concerned, it's for Phillip as much as for all those skeletons they found in the mass grave. You go on home. I'll be along soon."

Aarya gave her sister an exaggerated shrug and began walking towards home. Tesha turned down Hazelwood Avenue, reminding herself that everything had been calm and ordinary when she had returned to claim the sword that morning of All Soul's Day. She still wondered what had happened to the demonic figure who had risen above the house during the fire. Everyone had been too concerned with rescuing Dylan to see whether it had dissipated or fallen back

164

into the house, or where it might have gone.

It had been Joseph who took the information they had uncovered to Mayor Renick. To his credit, the mayor had organized an excavation and brought in archaeologists to assess the history of the site. With proof that it had been a crossroads where criminals were hung and subsequently buried combined with the investigation of the recent deaths, they had dug all the way to bedrock, uncovering the communal grave after finding the charred remains of Jerry Applegate. There had been no sign of Phillip's body or of that other man, Williamson, whom she had seen fall among the snakes.

Having learned that many of the 'criminals' who had been hung on the site were women accused of witchcraft, the memorial statue had simply been dedicated to all who had died on this site. Tesha had smiled when she first learned of the inscription. At least her best friend had been included.

Tesha wondered what had happened to all the snakes. She knew that at least some of them would hibernate in the winter and looked suspiciously at Mrs. Elwin's hedge as she crossed to the other side of the street. She wasn't surprised to see that the whole property at Number 23 had been paved over. Now the county wouldn't have to worry about maintenance. They had even placed a few park benches, though it was doubtful anyone would ever sit on them.

She walked up to the memorial, placed in the center of where the charred remains of the house had likely been leveled before pouring the cement. It was a statue of a woman, in honor of the innocent women who had been convicted of witchcraft. Tesha couldn't help thinking it resembled the ghostly woman she and Raymond had encountered. She laid the flowers at the foot of the statue and let her tears for Phillip fall freely now.

Distant thunder rolled across the overcast sky at the same moment, making her flinch. *A winter storm coming in, nothing more,* she thought.

Just as she was about to turn and walk towards home, she heard a voice.

"Tesha!"

She whirled around and looked at the statue suspiciously. She was sure the voice sounded like Phillip's. She heard it again, louder this time.

"Tesha, help me! I can't get out!"

Tesha opened her mouth, undecided whether it was to speak or to scream, when an ear-splitting shriek sounded from Mrs. Elwin's hedged yard across the road and reverberated into the darkening clouds.

If you enjoyed this book, please write a review on Amazon, Goodreads or any other book sites you frequent to share with other readers what you liked about it! Reviews help readers make decisions about the books that will suit them best, and even just a few words can be invaluable feedback to both author and reader.

The Author

Austin Crawley has always had an interest in the supernatural and macabre. He has a particular interest in real life ghost stories and spends his holidays visiting places that are reported to be haunted.

When he isn't dealing in spooks, he deals in the buying, selling and cutting of gemstones. On odd Tuesdays he convinces himself that it's because he was reincarnated from a pirate.

Blog: https://austincrawleyblog.wordpress.com/

Facebook: https://www.facebook.com/Austin-Crawley-687952104674224/

Twitter: https://twitter.com/austinocrawley

Also from Austin Crawley

A Christmas Tale

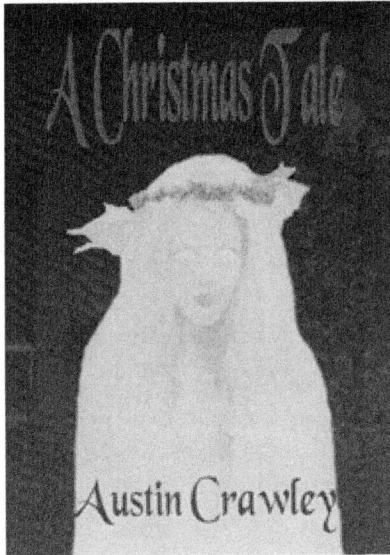

Few Christmas stories hold as much fascination as the story, A Christmas Carol by Charles Dickens.

Inspired by the Dickens tale, three young women decide to hold a séance to raise the spirits of Christmas Past, Present and Future. They don't expect a result, but what they call out of the aethyr gives them a creepy holiday they will never forget, if they live to tell the tale!

Sample

In her half-sleep confusion, Brittany turned to look whether the pizza box was still on the coffee table, then opened her mouth in a silent scream. Just beyond the coffee table, a luminescent figure floated just above the floor, staring at her through completely blank, white eyes. The figure resembled a ghostly little girl with hair as white as her gown and deathly white skin, but it was the lack of iris or pupil in those glowing eyes that most drew Brittany's horrified gaze.

The ghostly entity was semi-transparent and Brittany could see the mantel piece and the large Christmas tree through her soft, white glow. Her babyish mouth was set in an astonished 'O', as if she had been surprised to find Brittany in the room rather than presenting a spectral anomaly herself.

Even more disturbing was the clear, reverberating voice of the child ghost. Her eerie, girlish tones all but sang inside Brittany's head, though the ghostly mouth barely moved.

"Why doest thou, who has known many sorrows, summon me to revisit past misfortune and woe? Has thy grief not found healing in time? Hast thou not come to acceptance of that which was lost?"

Tears streamed down Brittany's face. An old wound, which she had thought long healed, reopened in stark, unforgiving clarity.

"No, please," she entreated the spirit. "Not that Christmas... we asked to see happy Christmases!"

Letters To The Damned

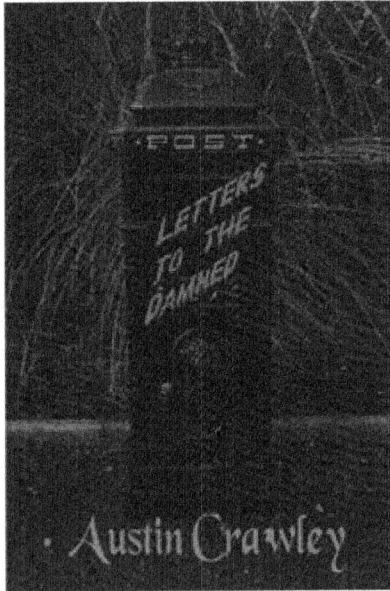

In a small English village, an abandoned black post box stands testament to the failing Royal Mail service where post box collections have ceased and letters must be delivered to the post office in the local shop.

However, the residents of this village continue to drop irregular letters into the black box. Messages to dead relatives are not only delivered, but often requests for supernatural intervention are acted upon in the world of the living where the dead and damned can only enter by special invitation.

When a visitor learns of the black post box, he dismisses it as local superstition and chides the villagers for their simple beliefs, until he accepts the challenge to test the box for himself. What would you ask for, if you could send a message to the damned?

A Spark of Justice

by J.D. Hawkins

A fatal accident in the lion tamer's cage at the circus sparks an insurance investigation that leads John Nieves, a former New York cop, to a list of possible murder suspects. His mission is to determine who had opportunity and motive to cause a wire to spark, aggravating a tiger just before the performance. It seems that The Great Rollo, beloved of millions, had enemies... both at the circus and among his own family.

All that is surreal and magical about the circus brings out some of Nieves' personal deepest fears, blinding him to the very real danger that is closer at hand. Nieves finds himself suppressing his innate fear of clowns to continue an investigation that by rights should have been wrapped up quickly. A series of near misses intrigues Nieves into looking deeper into the closed society of the circus and the secrets they are obviously going to great lengths to hide.

Printed in Dunstable, United Kingdom

70432666R00100